"I appreciate your altruism, *Miri*, but I'm not a man used to disappointing. I'm certain there is a way I can make up for it, and when the time comes, it will be done. In the meantime, call me Benjamin."

It was impossible that the innuendo she heard in his words could be anything but imaginary.

They both knew what was at stake.

But if someone had told her that she would be on a first-name basis with Benjamin Silver to kick off Hanukkah, she would have responded that *that* would have been a miracle.

If they had said she would be drinking exquisite rosé, reminiscing and making revealing confessions to him, then she would have called security to have them removed.

The idea of it alone was almost as ludicrous as the fact that she could have sworn she saw the same realizations mirrored in his own eyes.

This was *Benjamin Silver*, her project supervisor and one of the richest men in the world.

He was not someone she could relax around.

And yet here she was.

Marcella Bell is an avid reader, a burgeoning beader, and a corvid and honeybee enthusiast with more interests than hours in the day. As a late bloomer and a yogini, Marcella is drawn to stories that showcase love's incredible power to inspire transformation—whether they take place in the vast landscapes of the West or imagined palaces and exotic locales. When not writing or wrangling her multigenerational household and three dogs, she loves to hear from readers! To reach out, keep up or check in, visit marcellabell.com.

Books by Marcella Bell

Harlequin Presents

The Queen's Guard

Stolen to Wear His Crown
His Stolen Innocent's Vow
Pregnant After One Forbidden Night

Pregnant Princesses

His Bride with Two Royal Secrets

Visit the Author Profile page
at Harlequin.com for more titles.

Marcella Bell

SNOWBOUND IN HER BOSS'S BED

Recycling programs
for this product may
not exist in your area.

ISBN-13: 978-1-335-58392-5

Snowbound in Her Boss's Bed

Copyright © 2022 by Marcella Bell

For questions and comments about the quality of this book,
please contact us at CustomerService@Harlequin.com.

Harlequin Enterprises ULC
22 Adelaide St. West, 41st Floor
Toronto, Ontario M5H 4E3, Canada
www.Harlequin.com

Printed in U.S.A.

SNOWBOUND IN HER BOSS'S BED

This book is dedicated to my Gold family.
Not everyone is so lucky in the family they marry.
I am eternally grateful to have become a part of yours.

CHAPTER ONE

Miriam Howard sucked in a quiet gasp as she took in the immense property below.

Her stomach did a somersault while the plane began its descent, as if she rode over a hill in a car, rather than coasted smoothly toward the runway below.

Even blanketed in a light sheet of snow as everything was now, or maybe because of that, the expanse of development stood out in sharp contrast against the ocean of forest it was nestled within.

She had never before seen a private residence so large—and she was from Los Angeles.

She had also never seen so much snow.

Both were more unnerving than impressive.

When she had been informed yesterday that she would be making the trip to Aspen this morning, she had assumed that she would be landing at a small private airport akin to the one from which she had taken off in LA only hours before.

Instead, while the runway below was indeed

small and private, it was not to an airport that the pilot delivered her, but to the far end of what she could only surmise was Benjamin Silver's Colorado compound.

Miri shivered, despite the comfortable cabin temperature of Mr. Silver's private jet.

Descending upon Mr. Silver's famously private sanctuary, she wondered if there was such a thing as *too much* money.

If Mr. Silver wasn't proof of the possibility, over the past twenty-four hours he'd done a fair job of making the case.

Prior to 4:45 p.m. yesterday, Miri had had no travel plans on her horizon.

Now she was moments away from landing at a private compound in the isolated forests outside of Aspen, Colorado on a private jet—all because of Mr. Silver.

She didn't imagine the facts that the trip was both inconvenient and undesired—she had evening plans for the first time since she'd been hired as the new events director for the Los Angeles Jewish Community Foundation two weeks ago— particularly mattered to Mr. Silver. He was a self-made billionaire, after all. It was unlikely that he'd made it as far as he had by prioritizing the desires and convenience of his underlings.

And an underling was most definitely what Miri was to him—even if he wasn't her direct boss.

She didn't report to him for day-to-day things,

but he was the board chair of the JCF, the *head* head honcho, and that meant that she—and everyone else on staff, when it came down to it— reported to him.

He could have any one of them fired at any time.

And, making matters worse for Miri in particular, while she didn't report to him, she was tasked with working directly under him to coordinate and execute her most important responsibility as events director: the annual fundraising gala.

She had to jump when he said jump, not just to impress him, but in order to get the job done. She unfortunately needed whatever time he made available to her.

And, if their brief phone call the day before was to be any indication, Miri had gotten the distinct impression that Mr. Silver's time was extremely limited—and that he didn't want to spend much of it with her.

Never mind whether or not I want to spend mine *with him*, she mentally grumbled.

But, as board chair, Mr. Silver was the board member assigned to liaise with her, as well as the one to give official approval for any of her plans.

They had to work together, and his time was worth more than hers.

Hence her impending arrival at his mountain fortress.

Calling the private residence a fortress would

have been a bit hyperbolic in most cases, but not here.

Fortress wasn't even truly enough to describe the compound. Really, even that word needed some kind of modifier. *Monstrous*, perhaps? Or maybe *gargantuan*?

The largest building was at least the size of a hotel.

How was it even possible that such a structure was a private residence?

Miri couldn't fathom a family actually living in such a huge structure, even a wealthy one.

With that much space, a family could go weeks without running into one another.

Her own family was large and close-knit, and they had always done fine with just three bedrooms and a finished garage.

And while it had been a long time since Miri had lived at home with all of them, her absence hadn't created any more space. Especially not when her siblings were out there busily populating the world with her plethora of nieces and nephews, all of whom were happy to take the place she'd left.

Now that she lived alone, her entire personal life fit easily within the confines of a microscopic one-bedroom apartment. She had a tiny kitchen, a shower rather than a bathtub, and a bedroom that was too small to fit anything over a full-size bed, and it was still sometimes too much space.

And what if it were just him, all alone out here in the snow?

Miri blinked to clear her mind of the image. It was eerie and lonesome, and the last thing she wanted to think about before spending time in his company.

A place this massive with no family or friends nearby would make a person wonder if *they* were a ghost haunting the halls.

Family—born into, reconstructed or completely made up—was what gave a person the strength needed to navigate landscapes that were vast and filled with pitfalls.

That was true whether the setting was the endless forestland of Colorado's mountains, or the concrete jungle of Los Angeles.

His success was a clear indication that he had successfully navigated his fair share of vast landscapes. There had to have been somebody around, quietly supporting that.

Therefore, she was glad she'd brought doughnuts.

She had taken the risk of waking early to pick them up from a place in Highland Park that everyone had been raving about on her way to the airport that morning.

While under normal circumstances she would not have brought doughnuts along with her to a last-minute meeting with a billionaire, the current context made it seem not only appropriate, but shrewd.

As opposed to what she had learned about the JCF's offices, where contributing to the break room's baked goods collection was not only considered professional but simply the right thing to do, she was not under the impression that sweet treats would impress Benjamin Silver.

She *did* think, however, that there was a chance they might impress his family—whoever they happened to be.

Their meeting was taking place on the first day of Hanukkah at his sprawling private residence; whoever was around would appreciate doughnuts.

Impressing everyone that she met while wearing the hat of events director was not simply a fun exercise to break the ice, nor an attempt to win friends—at least not yet.

Her job was on the line.

She was only two weeks into her new position, a position that was critical to her being able to pay her rent.

To compound the pressure, she had barely secured the position in an extremely competitive hiring process in which she had been neither the favorite nor the most experienced candidate.

But—the result of her being desperate, loaded with more degrees and certifications than any one person had any business having, and inexperienced enough to be foolhardy—she had promised something that the other candidates had said couldn't be done.

She had promised that she could pull off this year's famed annual gala even though the date was only two months away and all the work that had been done up to her hiring had imploded in the fallout of a scandal.

She had projected confidence in making her promises, sensing that she had the hiring committee's attention.

The JCF had been planning to announce the cancellation of the gala.

And so they had taken her up on her bet, provisionally hiring her on the spot—the provision being that she delivered on her promise and gave them a gala the likes of which would make the community forget all about the fact that the former executive director and events director had both been fired upon the discovery of their years-long office affair.

The JCF was still reeling from the fallout among its community of supporters, their faith in the administration of the organization at an all-time low.

Only something transformative could distract and redirect their attention and restore their confidence.

Miri had promised a gala that would be just that.

So she needed Mr. Silver not just on her side, but behind her with full support.

She needed him wrapped around her little finger when it came to ideas and plans—at least if she had any hope of preserving her job.

Unfortunately, she was not off to a great start when it came to the billionaire, whom she had only been able to speak to for the first time yesterday—after emailing and reaching out to him multiple times a day every business day for the past two weeks.

Even more unfortunately, the moment had not been at her best.

"Virtual meetings leave questions, and I don't have time for follow-up calls," the man on the other end of the line had said in the kind of voice that narrated women's fantasies.

Deep and smooth, each perfectly modulated word vibrated with power and wealth.

Even, apparently, when he was being unreasonable.

Miri held back her frustrated sigh.

That he felt that way was a problem. As the board liaison assigned to the annual gala, Mr. Silver was the man she needed to work with.

He also currently resided outside of Aspen in Colorado, whereas she was operating out of the foundation's primary offices in Los Angeles.

"I have two hours to spare for this," he'd continued, the smooth chords of his words reaching through to the phone to once again wrap around her. "And that means we need to get it all done in one go, rather than meet virtually or exchange a thousand emails."

As gorgeous as it sounded, he chastised her with his mention of emails—of which she had sent many—before carrying on with his baritone bulldozing.

"You're going to fly out here tomorrow morning. We will spend a couple of hours making necessary calls and final preparations for the gala, and then you'll fly home. You will have the rare privilege of my complete attention, after which I don't expect to hear from you again until we meet again on the night of the gala."

Nothing about his suggestion was at all reasonable.

The following day, the day he was proposing they meet in person, was the first day of Hanukkah. And as if that weren't enough reason not to demand a sudden meeting, Miri already had a full day scheduled. Not to mention the fact that, in keeping with the tradition they'd started in their undergraduate days, she and her closest friends were getting together in the evening to celebrate the holiday.

These days they saw one another so infrequently, she didn't relish the possibility of missing it due to travel snafus.

Plus, getting tickets and a car rental at this stage would be an expensive nightmare—even if it was going on her business credit card.

But, smiling through her slightly locked jaw, Miri had said, "I'd be happy to fly out to Aspen, Mr. Silver. I'll coordinate travel immediately."

On the other end of the phone line, Mr. Silver had laughed.

"That's adorable, but no. Do you know how long it would take you just to get through the airport, let alone get a seat on a commercial plane at this time of year? I did mention that I have just two hours, did I not? It would take you that much time just to get to my home from the airport via car. No. You'll take my plane. Are you ready for my airport's address?"

"Sir, really, it's no trouble," Miri had pressed back.

She didn't even like sharing rides around town. The idea of being at the mercy of someone's plane for out-of-state travel sat even less well with her. If she was doing this at all, she was making her own arrangements.

"The flight from LA to Aspen is not long and I don't mind a red-eye," she'd added.

Miri hated to feel indebted to or reliant on anyone—especially for the experience of a luxury that she hadn't asked for. When you owed people, they had a hard time allowing you to change.

If Miri was going to pull this gala off, she needed him to be open to change.

Irritation energized Mr. Silver's voice, but the edge of it only enhanced its spine-tingling nature.

Voices like his belonged in the entertainment industry, not on the board of directors for a non-profit organization.

"I told you we don't have the time," he'd said, with a firmness to his words that set off a little flame of defiance in Miriam.

He wasn't the only one who was irritated.

"Private planes are far more likely to crash," she said drily. "I imagine my death would create a bigger delay than the cab ride from the airport to your home office."

Then she'd clapped a silent hand over her mouth.

Exasperation had momentarily clouded her good judgment.

She was going to get herself fired.

The last thing she needed was to give the impression that she was difficult, or, God forbid, *sassy.*

Either alone could spell death for a Black woman in high-level nonprofit work.

Mr. Silver, however, had surprised her.

He'd laughed.

The sound was as rich, warm and well-rounded as his speaking voice, but unlike his voice, the modulated and controlled cadence of which sounded like money, his laugh was the open joy of a regular person, rolling out of him as if he could recall what it was like to go to grocery stores and pay parking tickets.

As if she had been joking, he came back with his own sarcasm and humor. "If you're so concerned about the plane, my helicopter is always available…"

"I'll pass on the helicopter offer, thank you," she said quickly, shuddering even at the idea while simultaneously relieved that it appeared that she hadn't put her foot in it after all.

Nonetheless, it had been time to get off the phone before something even more disastrous happened.

"I'll be at the location you gave me in the morning," she said.

"Excellent. I'll see you tomorrow. And don't worry, you have my word that you'll be back in Los Angeles long before dark, no risk of missing even a moment of Hanukkah with your family. Two hours, no more."

He had hung up without saying goodbye, and at the click, Miriam had let out a sigh of relief.

She could have told him that that particular concern was unnecessary because, while she had a family, they wouldn't be celebrating any holidays with her any time soon and her friends wouldn't mind her being late—but did not.

Benjamin Silver had no reason to care about her personal life.

The only thing he cared about was getting everything they had to get through done in two hours, and if they were going to do that, she had a lot of prep work to do.

Fortunately, that meant a lot to distract her from the fact that she would be attending a meeting with the sixth-richest man in the world.

A long night in front of the computer had to be enough to dull the stress of the idea.

They would meet for no more than two hours, and then she could return home, that much closer to securing her position with the JCF and done with Mr. Silver.

The next day had arrived very quickly, though, and now, as the plane touched down, Miri wasn't sure if her reassurances might have been a bit premature.

Staring in awe at the wintery world outside the comfortable private jet, she was reminded that, in truth, her time with Mr. Silver had not even begun.

CHAPTER TWO

"A CARDIGAN?" he asked incredulously, adding, "You thought it was a good idea to wear a cardigan on a business trip to Colorado in November?"

Exasperation was just one of many emotions Benjamin Silver felt upon laying eyes on Ms. Miriam Howard. Among the surge, however, exasperation was the most straightforward and direct.

He preferred communication that was clear and to the point.

Therefore, he made it clear what he thought of the cardigan.

While the snow was just a light blanket over the ground this early in the year, it was, nonetheless, *snow*.

Closing his eyes, he exhaled through his nose, allowing himself a respite from the effort of not devouring her with his eyes.

Her appearance had somewhat stunned him.

When he focused on the cardigan, however, rather than the fact that her figure and face would have made the proud subjects of a sensual oil painting, he could handle himself.

She stood above average height, which appealed to him as a tall man, and had glowing skin that looked soft enough to touch.

And she wore a cardigan to Colorado in November, he reminded himself.

And in what should have been a more compelling fact, she was his subordinate.

Ms. Howard had been an emergency hire. This was their first meeting.

His reaction was inappropriate.

But she was nothing like what he had expected.

A cardigan, he repeated mentally.

Taking her in, he wondered if the foundation had simply added fuel to the fire that was this year's gala in selecting her for the position of events director.

She looked incredibly young, her clear brown skin bright and dewy, even in the crisp dry mountain air of Colorado.

She certainly did not present the kind of mild-mannered mid-career executive image that would have reassured their supporters that the JCF had left its sexy and salacious days behind it.

She was the sexiest woman he had ever encountered.

Even in budget business attire, she gave the impression of lushness.

Shaking himself, he wrestled his mind back to the cardigan.

And, young though she might look, it wasn't a naive newbie who answered him when she finally spoke. Her irritation obvious in the words that squeezed through her clenched teeth, she said, "I was under the impression that we would be meeting inside."

She might be inexperienced, he acknowledged, *but she has spine.*

She revealed it now, as she had when they'd spoken on the phone the day before.

If anyone knew how far spine could take a person in this world, it was him.

He'd built an empire on spine.

If she possessed enough of it, she might even be able to deliver on the bold promises she had made to the hiring committee.

Her cardigan, however, did not convey spine.

It conveyed poor planning, and planning was her job.

"It's November. In Aspen," he said, giving her no quarter even as he allowed her stubborn streak to impress him.

In response, her stunning topaz eyes narrowed, flashing against the warm brown backdrop of her skin.

He had never seen eyes like hers before—warm whiskey, rimmed with deep obsidian.

"Forgive me for not packing my skis," she retorted.

Flushed heat then came to the satiny apples of her cheeks, bringing a subtle duskiness to their warm expanse, and the pressure in Benjamin's veins ticked up a notch not for the first time since he had been in her presence.

Perhaps that reaction was what was behind the pleasure he found in goading her.

A part of him recognized her as a woman worth romantic pursuit.

The remainder of him, however, was committed to the success of the annual gala.

And attraction to the new events director, after what had happened with the previous, was entirely inappropriate for that goal.

Even if she was nearly six feet tall in the heels she wore and had the curves to carry it.

Benjamin tore his mind away from her body and returned it to her clothing.

Clothing was innocuous and safe.

Her outfit consisted of a blouse buttoned low enough to give hints of what looked like a lace-edged beige satin camisole beneath, both of which were tucked neatly at the narrow waist of her black pencil skirt.

Her heels were skinny and also black. And to bring it all together, she wore her ridiculous, flimsy beige cardigan.

Everything she wore was thin.

And she was carrying a bright teal box.

A faint smile coming to his lips, Benjamin replied smoothly, "I've got plenty of skis, if it comes to it. What I haven't got—" the edge returned to his words "—are spare women's parkas."

Though, of course, between the staff and his guest supplies, Benjamin would not have been surprised to learn that he *did* have spare parkas.

"I'm sure I'll survive," Ms. Howard replied smoothly, her voice as dry and cold as the air around them, and Benjamin nearly chuckled.

Her sartorial wisdom might be questionable, but she was funny.

And she had backbone.

The traits could only help her get her job done—as long as she knew how to create the kinds of events that schmoozed wealthy donors like himself into opening their wallets.

Getting started toward that end was why he had driven out to the runway to pick her up himself, rather than send someone.

He had not braved the elements in order to criticize her choice in clothing, but in order to get working.

But with her teeth chattering as they got in the car, he instead turned the heat up and yet again adjusted his expectations.

Ms. Howard was necessitating quite the number of adjustments.

She was nothing like what he had pictured when he'd spoken to her on the phone yesterday.

Her Southern California accent was so reminiscent of the women he'd gone to school with as a suburban kid in Los Angeles that he'd assigned her a figure and persona to match.

Instead, stealing a glance at her through the corner of his eye as he drove them to his home, Benjamin could not remember ever meeting a single woman who looked like the one currently riding in his passenger seat.

Certainly not the entire package she presented—the remarkable eyes, the height, the willingness to push back at him.

Currently, she thrummed with a swirling blend of righteous indignation and professional poise he found mildly impressive.

Pulling into the circular driveway at the front entrance of the closest thing he had to a home anymore, he smiled when she let out a little gasp.

He was proud of his getaway in the trees, though no one had ever visited it.

The compound was a testament to all of the hard work he had done in his life to get there.

Going around the car, he opened her door and offered her his hand.

She took it, stepping outside to take the structure in.

Her palm slid into his, cool and smooth with a whisper of something that had him leaning in to hear before he had the presence of mind to pull back.

Ms. Howard did not appear to notice his proximity, however, her attention instead focused on his home.

The front entrance had been designed to inspire wonder, and it appeared to have done the job with Ms. Howard.

Her heavily lashed almond eyes widened as she stared.

The enormous building boasted beams that seemed to have to have come from trees from another epoch, their incredible girths anchored into equally massive rounded river stone bases. The real estate listing had described it as "an elegant log and stone cabin on a large private forested property outside of Aspen," highlighting its classic exposed-beam design, vaulted ceilings and rich natural materials.

He'd purchased it on sight, feeling instant ease with its immensity and lack of facade.

Growing up in a city that grew illusions, he had longed for authenticity.

It pleased him that Ms. Howard was impressed.

Closing her car door behind her, he then led her through the front door and into the vast foyer with its wall of floor-to-ceiling windows that stared out into miles and miles of forest.

To offset some of the heavy, closed-in feeling that log cabins—even enormous ones—

could sometimes have, he'd had his designers incorporate white accent walls of smooth adobe throughout the home, their rough natural surfaces blending well with the thick rounded beams of the mountain estate.

He had also added more than two dozen new windows and skylights to the existing impressive number, brightening the interior and bringing even more of the vast forest into the many hallways, dining rooms and sitting rooms that he now led her through.

He did not give her a tour, though.

As much as he was enjoying her little noises of astonishment and awe, she was not here to look at his house.

She was here to work.

To that end, passing several sitting and specialty rooms and hallways without comment, he brought her to his office.

Located in the deep interior of the sprawling chalet, Benjamin's office was connected to his personal suite via thick French doors that were currently closed.

He had had the private wing of the cabin remodeled to meet his exact specifications, including the office.

The desk was his preferred height, built into a bay of windows that overlooked the forest.

Built-in bookshelves lined the walls, fabricated

to the exact size required to house his favorite works.

A fireplace and seating area were set up in the corner for his comfort.

His office space was more closed in and cozier than much of the home, which he preferred.

Closed-in and cozy reminded him of where he had come from. It connected him to the drives of a younger, poorer version of himself.

His office reminded him that he had achieved what he had because it had been his parents' dream that the world know his name—not because he was trying to be someone he was not.

Whether he was one of the most powerful men in the world or, as he had been when they were alive to bear witness, one of the most anonymous—he knew who he was and he was comfortable with it.

Ms. Howard, however, appeared to be less moved by his most revealing space than she had been by the rest of the house.

She likely saw only that it was less awe-inspiring than the other areas, not realizing that it represented the essence of him.

To her, in all likelihood, it was merely the room that housed a desk and computer.

She wouldn't necessarily see that the computer and what he did with it were worth more than the entire compound—as well as the reason he could afford it all in the first place.

"This is where we'll be working," he said, observing her as he spoke. "You can sit there."

He pointed to a chair at his left.

Ms. Howard nodded and went to the seat, placing her teal box on the desk to the side of her shoulder bag.

The bag had seen better days.

Unlike the foundation's previous events director, a woman who had owned a seemingly endless supply of immaculate designer briefcases and handbags, Ms. Howard's accessory had cracks in the leather of its handles and fraying seams.

In fact, like the rest of her attire, it appeared rather threadbare.

"What's in the box?" he asked, unable to keep a taut note from entering his voice as he took a seat at her side.

"Oh," she said, taking a quick glance at the box as if she had momentarily forgotten about it. "Doughnuts from Grease Monkey. It's the new *it* spot in LA."

Lifting a brow, he remained silent, staring at her for a moment before smirking at the direction of his thoughts.

She would have no idea bringing doughnuts would touch a nerve.

She was probably just eager to impress.

"Do you usually go through a box of doughnuts in a two-hour meeting?"

A frown swept across her brow at his question. "Absolutely not."

He chuckled. "So they're for me, then?"

Shaking her head in another quick negative, Ms. Howard denied quickly once again, "No."

"Then who were you hoping to impress with doughnuts from LA's latest hot spot?"

Frown deepening, Ms. Howard looked around as if she expected someone to appear in the deep inner sanctum of his house. "They're for your family. With the holidays kicking off tonight, I thought…"

Benjamin stilled.

She had brought doughnuts for the loved ones that she assumed he would be around for the holidays.

It was a sweet gesture.

There was just no one left in the world that he loved.

He had been blessed with two sets of adoring parents in his life—and he had lost them both.

Neither set had left him with any grandparents, cousins, aunts or uncles, and being twice orphaned had left him leery of going for a third shot and making a family of his own.

And if all of that meant an isolated existence for him, it also meant there was no family to compete with his work for his time.

There was no one to make demands of him, no one to disappoint.

He could disappear into the woods and no one would come looking for him.

He could lose himself in work and no one would find him.

But, of course, she wouldn't know any of that.

And he intended to keep it that way.

Mystery was more powerful than pity.

For anyone to pity him was absurd.

He had been blessed with more love, happiness and success in a single lifetime than the vast majority of humans on the planet.

What did it matter if all that remained now was success?

Concealing his thoughts behind a polite smile, Benjamin did not answer the unspoken question about his family. Instead, he commented, "Thoughtful of you. Obvious, but thoughtful."

Ms. Howard whipped around to face him, her eyes widening at him in offense in the process.

He wanted her offended. Offended was better than curious about his life.

She opened her mouth, but he spoke before she could. "I've buzzed my assistant to retrieve them. I'm sure they'll be appreciated."

He did not mention by whom.

She need not know they would simply be set out for his staff to enjoy at a later time.

"Shall we get started, Ms. Howard?" he asked.

She gave a decisive nod, then reached into her bag to pull out a dinosaur of a laptop. Setting up in front of her, she opened the ancient device and began a slow process of starting it up and loading programs. "What's the Wi-Fi password?" she asked without looking at him, and Benjamin was amused.

He appreciated these brief moments in which she seemed to forget just who he was and treated him like a colleague, as opposed to her wealthy supervisor.

He answered her question as he continued to observe her.

She opened impressive, color-coded spreadsheets, electronic brochures and a number of emails.

Her fingers flew across her keyboard at an administrative clip, her well-shaped nails just long enough to click against the keys.

Her hands were softly padded and elegant, her simple manicure tasteful if not of the highest end, fingers moving with confidence and assuredness.

She continued to prepare, focused on the work in front of her, until his assistant arrived to remove the doughnuts.

At the interruption, Ms. Howard looked up with a smile and a warm, "Thank you."

As she spoke, her cheeks lifted, her entire countenance brightening with the expression, and Benjamin found himself momentarily surprised, right alongside his assistant.

That Ms. Howard's smile was enough to stop

even his hatchet assistant in her tracks, an aging mountain woman who utterly lacked a sense of romance, spoke to its power.

Turning to Benjamin, Ms. Howard's expression transitioned to one of focused seriousness, her eyebrows drawn slightly together as she asked, "Where would you like to begin, Mr. Silver?"

But though he had recovered from her arresting smile, Benjamin nonetheless did not answer her immediately.

Before that, he slid out the chair beside her and took it, reaching forward to press the subtle round button in the desk's surface. Soundlessly, a panel in the center of the desk opened and his large, thin monitor rose from its compartment within the desk.

"Let's begin with the venue," he said before booting up his own system with the voice command, "Load!"

The system, and the wealth of very proprietary coding contained within it, was programmed to respond only to his voice. For additional security, his keypad, which rose from its own panel within the desk at his word, responded to his fingerprints alone.

He was a man who appreciated his privacy, his security and his world programmed exclusively to himself.

Fortunately, he had enough money to ensure all three.

With his system up and running, he turned back to Ms. Howard, covering the strange jolt he had felt each time he laid eyes on her with a frown.

"Where are we with that? Concept? Progress? All of it in two minutes," he commanded.

Frown flashing across her own face, Ms. Howard turned her gaze to the many tabs, images and pdfs open on the screen in front of her. With a faint shake of her head her eyes flashed from detail to detail, the wheels of her mind obviously turning as she bent herself to the unexpected task of trying to so succinctly summarize the bulk of her work for the foundation thus far.

Benjamin, however, did not modify his request.

If she could not summarize her efforts, she did not have command of the situation.

Could she deliver?

When her eyelids lifted there was a steady resolve in her bright amber orbs.

Her gaze, direct and clear as it was, rattled him, shaking him as if she had some power to influence the tectonic plates of his subconscious, but he processed the impact in the back of his mind, keeping his primary focus trained on her full lips.

Moistening them before she spoke, she said, "I reserved Vibiana. They're full service and since time is short, I thought it best to take them up on that. Because it's a decommissioned cathedral, it's got a lot of very old-world European detail, so I have been conceptualizing a Secret Garden theme.

I looked through previous files and it has never been done before. It's pretty and festive, but still far from Christmassy. Picture lovely architecture and detail, mosaics, greenery all around. There is also an outdoor garden area that will serve as the ballroom floor, so to speak."

Her ideas were fresh, possibly exciting—as long as they were carried off with taste as opposed to kitsch. They were certainly nothing like anything the foundation had done before.

There was a big gap between a good idea and a solid execution, however.

"You're telling me the plan is to gather the city's wealthiest Jews together in a Roman Catholic cathedral?" he pushed.

Had she thought her plan through, or was she merely carried away in imagery? Did she understand what was at stake, or did she think this event was merely an opportunity to plan an almost-wedding?

Her frown deepening, Ms. Howard repeated and emphasized her first word when she spoke. "*Decommissioned* and now one of the trendiest event spots downtown, so yes, it is. The location is ideal, the full service and reputation for excellent catering is beyond a time-saver, and the capacity is exactly what we need for this event. It's large enough for the dinner service, while also offering private and intimate spaces for smaller groups to gather and converse. Honestly, it's better than we could have hoped for. That they could even fit us into their calendar was a matter of dumb luck and cancellation. They have a kosher kitchen, and the chef is well versed. I really can't see how we could have done better, especially given the circumstances."

Benjamin appreciated her thinking, though he continued to search out any flaws in her ideas.

"It's not the Getty," he said.

Letting out a little noise of frustration, Ms. Howard's response was both sharper and quicker than her previous. "No. It's not the Getty. And, as I've discussed with the rest of the senior staff, as well as some of the more involved donors who somehow got word, given the situation we're presently dealing with, not to mention the fact that it is now absolutely unavailable to us, the Getty is unfortunately no longer an option on the table."

There was that interesting spine of hers again.

Benjamin allowed a small smile to tilt the corners of his mouth upward. "That's a rather politic way to describe a scandal," he said.

Ms. Howard gave an unconcerned shrug. "My job is to ensure that the foundation's events continue to run smoothly, now and into the future. I'm not interested in rehashing the past."

"Well said," Benjamin replied, "and, as *I* said, politic."

The previous events director had been fired due

to the revelation of her ongoing affair with the foundation's married executive director.

Fraternizing between employees was prohibited at the JCF.

Both actors had been fired, deeply damaging the reputation of the foundation and rattling community faith in its capacity to carry out its mission.

Ms. Howard wasn't the only new hire, nor the most important.

But, as opposed to Ms. Howard, the hiring committee had gone with the most experienced and proven candidate for executive director in order to re-instill faith in the community and steer the organization through the rocky transition.

The former executive director had bowed to the decisions of the board, cooperating and supporting it with as much grace as she could.

The former events director, however, had not been so accommodating.

Choosing vengeance, she had taken her contacts with her when she left as well as sullied the foundation's name among her network of service providers.

And after fifteen years in the position, the woman's network had been extensive.

In attesting to have the skill to clean up the mess, the newly hired Ms. Howard had agreed to not just race against the clock, but to buck the flow of how things were normally done.

The foundation's largest donors, however, did not tend to be fans of bucking the flow.

"You're going to need that when we announce a new venue," Benjamin added.

If she had been comfortable around him, she might have sighed in commiseration. Her eyes said as much, even while outwardly she merely held herself still and took a long blink.

"I've gathered as much," she said. "At this point, though, I have sampled menu options and walked the space myself, so I am confident that the experience will change hearts and minds."

"And what about those who will refuse outright? This is LA we're talking here. Never put it past people to simply not be willing to drive downtown."

Without missing a beat, Ms. Howard replied, "That's where you come in. This year it is more important than ever that you reach out to our most important donors with personal invitations. I can give them a gala they won't forget, but you need to sell it."

Benjamin held back a full smile after getting yet another glimpse of the steel in her.

She had communicated the same message, earnestly and with urgency, in the many emails she had sent him. Though she did not realize it, he had done better than respond to an electronic message. He had given her his direct time.

He wanted this to succeed as much as she did.

"Ah, yes," he said, warmth cracking some of the hard lines of his face. "A personal invitation from the billionaire. Well, if I am to whore myself out, it's likely time to get into the details."

"So I have your approval for the venue and theme?" she confirmed.

She needed it—his approval—and so he knew she listened for his response carefully. It appeared she was the type of person unwilling to jump to conclusions.

He appreciated the trait.

It revealed that she was keenly aware of the time constraints she was working within and would not risk losing any to mistakes or misunderstandings.

He nodded, confirming with a "yes" but no further elaboration. She need not know that not only did he approve, but that he found her ideas a refreshing change from the glitz and glam aesthetic of previous years.

Ms. Howard's eyes lit with a spark of real joy. "Excellent. Now, for food. Given the time frame, it seemed best to go tried and true for the menu, sticking with the chef's most popular option of a three-course meal with seafood, red meat and vegetarian options, fruit and chocolate dessert selections, and a very open bar. If you agree, it's a simple matter of letting the chef know—"

Stopping her, Benjamin held up a hand. "What are the options?" he asked.

"Salmon, filet mignon and vegetable risotto," she answered, eyebrows drawing together as she looked from her screen to him.

Benjamin shook his head. "No. Absolutely not. Your concept thus far has been interesting and fresh. I expected better from the menu. The donors will, too."

"Excuse me," she said, her right brow lifting slightly, arguments reading themselves in her eyes. "It's my judgment that with the event less than four weeks away we don't have the time to experiment with a menu and the subsequent tastings. The classics done right blow people away, time and again."

"No," Benjamin repeated, more certain he was right with every word he heard. "If we give them what they might have delivered to their doorstep on any given Tuesday night, the letdown will be what people talk about afterward, no matter how many pretty flowers you surround them with. Your menu bears no relationship to the concept. By that alone, it breaks the continuity of the evening and theme, makes it clear that the recent scandal was a sign that the foundation is indeed faltering and disorganized. It is more critical this year than ever that every detail reflect competence or they're not going to hand over their money. Anything that hints at haphazard or thrown together at the last minute will have lasting impacts. And more than that, it's boring. Give me something better. That idea is lazy and below your standard."

That idea is lazy and below your standard...

The words rang in Miri's head, stunning in their blunt censure—even if they were true.

How dare he say so? What did he know of her standards?

The classic catering offering idea *had* been lazy—intentionally—because Miriam had seen the menu as the best place to save time in the miracle she was trying to pull off.

There simply wasn't time to reinvent the wheel, and food was a place where people preferred the usual.

Or so she had determined.

Mr. Silver clearly did not agree.

Unable to fully hide the faint edge to her tone, Miri said, "I apologize, but I'm going to need you to clarify. Are you asking me to come up with a new menu right now?"

He nodded impatiently. "It appears I was crystal clear. What you've got now is basic and has nothing to do with your theme."

Miri pressed back. "I won't argue those points. It was a sacrifice I felt was warranted considering our time constraints."

With a dismissive snort, Mr. Silver waved her words away like so many excuses. "I don't care what your reasons were. I told you to do better."

Miri's mouth dropped open.

The man was out of his mind and mad with power. It was the only explanation—for any element of her day, honestly, from the unrequested flight to the fancy desktop, to this right now.

How dare he speak to her like a child?

Like he was some kind of mentor pressuring her into higher performance.

And this was *after* all of his comments about her cardigan.

Thank God they were only meeting for two hours. And that she had a night with her closest friends to look forward to when it was all over.

He's been complimentary of the concept thus far, a timid internal voice offered.

Miriam stamped that voice out.

The last thing this man needed was someone inside *her* head making excuses for him.

Autocratic, bad-mannered, out of touch, toxic man... Her mental litany continued as she forced her face into a smile.

"Why certainly, Mr. Silver. Recalling that the theme is Secret Garden, we should obviously have a menu built around lush produce prepared simply with fresh herbs, botanical cocktails, and desserts inspired by the overflowing bounty of a summer garden, throwing in honey berry drizzles and edible flowers here and there throughout it all for the whimsy. Is that more along the lines of what you were thinking?" She said it all brightly, but the flat tone of her voice said exactly what she thought.

She thought he was being outrageous. Everything about him.

His demands, his mountain fortress, his power, his ability to make her forget that everything depended on making a good impression with him and instead respond with a more authentic version of herself—all of it.

Without his cooperation, there was no way she would keep her job. Without her job, the only place she had to go was back home. Pride had pushed her to stay in her car the two weeks immediately after graduation rather than go back to her family home before she'd gotten her apartment, but she knew she didn't have enough pride for a second round of that.

She would rather do whatever it took to keep her apartment and the new job she was already in love with.

She wanted those things more than she was interested in chasing any wild thoughts she might be inclined to think about Mr. Benjamin Silver.

He might be good-looking and have a great voice, but he also lived on a different planet from the one she inhabited. He was entirely out of her league—both because of the foundation and because of his wealth.

He was not a man she could afford to be a more authentic version of herself with.

He was a man she had to be the sharpest, most impressive version of herself with.

He held her gaze for a moment silently, his clear blue eyes dancing with a light that could have been temper or humor.

It flashed through her mind that under different circumstances, she wouldn't have minded knowing him well enough to know the difference.

Then he smiled, slowly, one corner of his mouth lifting at a time, offering Miri a glimpse of his straight white teeth, and she had her answer: humor.

Even as she attempted to shore up the foundation of her professionalism, his grinning eyes promised he could handle a little pushback.

"Exactly," he said. "Much better, Ms. Howard." He continued to grin as he elongated the *Ms.* in a way that could only be interpreted as insolence. "That's much more in alignment with the event you've put together thus far."

"I'll update it accordingly, sir," she said, exhaling through flared nostrils with irritation even as a part of her was pleased at what was ultimately a show of real buy-in to her plan.

Here again was the contrary sense of humor that she had encountered on the phone.

He joked, but he was also serious.

He meant every word he said, even when his delivery was shameless.

Sighing out the last of her irritation on the

point, she updated her spreadsheet, elaborating and specifying the menu she had rattled off to him facetiously.

Eyeing the updated menu with narrowed eyes, a part of her grumbled, knowing the necessary tastings would have to be squeezed into her already tight schedule.

The rest of her acknowledged that the revision was an improvement over the original.

With his input, the new menu was more interesting and memorable, and far more aligned with her concept.

"Wonderful work, Ms. Howard. Now that's sorted, please continue. I believe we had arrived at entertainment."

He spoke as if he were a king, generously doling out his approval, and Miri resisted the urge to roll her eyes.

She didn't know why it was so hard to maintain control of her reactions when it came to the man at her side.

It was probably just that everything he said and did was provoking.

If he could have managed to stop behaving as if the entire world worked for him for more than three minutes, it might have been easier to keep a handle on herself.

Never mind that she *did* work for him.

They continued through the remaining elements of the gala in generally the same manner—Mr.

Silver waving his dismissive hand of approval to most of what she presented with periodic breaks for criticism that goaded her into improvement.

That he seemed to understand her intentions without needing explanations only made it that much more irritating each time he lambasted the elements of her plans that were merely acceptable or expedient.

But to both of their credits, the event improved at each and every point at which he stopped her.

When they were done, Miriam was confident that if this gala didn't blow its attendees away, it would be because those attendees were dead inside.

Unfortunately, her neck was also stiff and tense from the effort it had taken to rein herself in every time her mind wanted to dash off on a wild tangent related to his voice or brace for his next critical interruption.

Bringing a hand to rub her neck, she checked her watch, only to startle at the time.

They were late—by an hour.

How had they gone over by a whole hour?

By the way Mr. Silver had gone on and on about how limited his time was, she would have expected him to have set an alarm to keep them on schedule.

As it was, going over the hour threatened to put even *her* off schedule.

Yes, flying by private jet saved a lot of time,

but losing an hour meant losing the chance to get home and change her clothes before she headed out to meet her friends.

But out loud, all she said was, "It looks like we've gone over our two hours."

She packed her things back into her bag with a new urgency.

"What?" His response was swift, that stunning voice of his filled with genuine and not exactly pleased surprise.

Even caught off guard it was kind of sexy.

Shocked at herself at the thought, Miri moved with even more purpose.

She needed to get out of Colorado and back to Los Angeles. A warm night with friends would wash this whole encounter away—which she obviously needed.

They might work well together, but she was grateful it wasn't going to be an all-the-time thing. Three hours in the company of Mr. Silver was simply more than her body and mind could handle.

Men were not supposed to both be as rich as he was and look the way he did.

Where was the equality in that?

He needed more flaws than the habit of delivering criticisms with the bluntness of a baseball bat.

He should not have been blessed with the kind of voice that belonged on television, nor should he have had the physical features to match.

He should not have had bright azure eyes, as clear as a glacier.

He should not have worn his hair long so that its soft mink-brown waves framed and feathered around his face and thick broad shoulders.

He should not have had full lips and straight dark brows, or his incredible height.

He was supposed to be an arrogant software guy approaching midlife.

Instead, he was attractive even when his behavior wasn't.

And after three hours that were supposed to have only been two, it had finally short-circuited her.

Miri was exhausted—by his energy, his exactitude, his commands, his gorgeousness and her reactions to it all.

For his part, Mr. Silver had the decency to look a bit worn himself.

Looking at his watch, he frowned, the expression flaring in his cool blue stare not the surprise of a man caught unawares by how much time had passed but the irritation of a man used to total control, especially over the clock.

He was offended that time had gotten away from him.

Well, good, Miri thought. *It's about time someone other than me was offended.*

"It cost an unexpected hour, but we made excellent headway." She didn't know why she made an attempt to comfort him when he could stand to be reminded that the elements didn't bend to his will, but she did, adding, "It will be just like you said on the phone. We won't need to connect again until the night of the gala."

He only nodded absently, frown still firmly in place, lost in his own thoughts.

Well, if he wasn't pleased with their progress and lack of need for further contact, Miri was.

They'd done good work, which, simple as it was, was something she took pride in.

She wasn't made for last-minute flights on private planes and private meetings with billionaires. She was made for working in an office with a shared break room that was always stocked with baked goods.

She was made for water coolers and event planning and proving her value by showing the funders a good time.

She was made for good work, intimate dinners with longtime friends, quiet nights at home curled up with a good book and finally establishing some real independence in her life.

In all of that, she was not, as the afternoon had made painfully obvious to her, equipped to withstand the onslaught of an ice king richer than most world leaders and hotter than an A-lister.

Was it any wonder she was losing control of her mind?

And to make matters worse, she still had to

brave the perilous and freezing journey through the snow to get back to Mr. Silver's plane and private runway.

Once she was on the plane, though, she would be able to breathe a sigh of relief away from the hawklike blue gaze of Mr. Benjamin Silver and focus on the warm and relaxing evening ahead of her.

Where, thank God, there will be wine, she reminded herself.

Miri sighed out loud in anticipation, and Mr. Silver gaze shot to her, a quizzical look in his eyes.

He really had the most arresting eyes.

Miriam would not have been surprised to learn he could see straight through everyone he encountered.

"Private joke?" he asked, leading her to the office door they'd entered not two, but three, hours before.

Shaking her head, Miriam said, "No. Just getting a little delirious. Air is thinner here," she added lightly.

Self-deprecating, he smirked. "Is that a nice way of saying I suck the oxygen out of a room?" he asked, and though she didn't know him well—at all, really—Miri knew he was joking.

She smiled and shook her head lightly but said no more.

From another man, the joke might have been

charming. But not from him. She couldn't allow him to be charming.

He was too powerful—had too much sway in her life to be charming from a safe distance.

Charm could be fun, but it was also dangerous.

Charm disarmed. It was fun and made you feel pretty, and it was also fickle and liable to abruptly leave you alone in a lurch.

She had an ex-high-school-sweetheart fiancé who had been charming until he wasn't, and the experience had taught her that charm was something she could allow into her life only under strict parameters.

Alone in the woods with a man with enough power to have the world literally at his fingertips, a face and physique that belonged on the silver screen, and a voice that made her want to take off her clothes—whether it was demanding more of her or calling her out or simply exchanging pleasantries—were not those parameters.

"This place is so big, inside and out. No single man could take up all the air. Is that why you like to spend so much time out here?"

He laughed, the sound deep and resonant, and Miri once again questioned her decisions.

Making him laugh was a bad idea.

"You've found me out," he said, still smiling, his eyes glittering like ice in the moonlight. "Here, even a man such as myself is humbled by the surroundings."

He was mesmerizing, like something beautiful because it was dangerous, and for a moment she was frozen looking at him.

It took her several seconds to shake free once more.

She had never encountered a man around whom walking the line was so exhausting.

And once again he was telling the truth even as he joked.

There was real respect for the awe-inspiring landscape in his humor.

When she had collected her things in her shoulder bag once more, he led her toward the office door. "Despite our additional hour, you should still arrive back in LA with plenty of time to spare before sundown."

Miriam nodded, relieved again at the prospect of a night celebrating Hanukkah with her friends after the intensity of her meeting with Mr. Silver.

Opening the door, he stepped aside to let her through, only to stop in his tracks upon finding his assistant standing on the other side of the door, a severe frown on her face.

"I'm sorry to be the bearer of bad news, sir," the woman said, without preamble or a hint of remorse in her voice and as blunt as her employer, "but a storm swept in. They're calling it a full-on blizzard. Chuck says he doesn't know when he'll be able to get back into the sky, but it's not going to be today."

Mr. Silver stilled. "There was no warning?" he asked, censure heavy in the question.

His assistant remained unfazed. "The do-not-disturb alert was on," the older woman replied with a shrug, as if that explained her not poking in to let them know of an impending storm that had the potential to prevent Miriam from getting home.

In response, however, Mr. Silver nodded, accepting the response as if it were perfectly reasonable.

But it was not reasonable.

It was completely unreasonable.

Blizzards weren't the kind of thing that happened to her.

They should have been warned. She needed to get home. To her friends, and the sun, and Los Angeles.

And most of all, she needed to get away from Mr. Benjamin Silver—before she did or said something to get herself fired.

CHAPTER THREE

"How long ago did it roll in?" Benjamin asked his assistant, irritation in his voice though none of it was for the messenger. He knew where the fault lay, and it wasn't with the bearer of bad news.

He had been very clear with his staff about his expectations when the do-not-disturb light above his office was lit. He was not to be disturbed— under any circumstances.

"About thirty-five minutes ago, sir," his assistant replied with her characteristic specificity.

It was exactly as he had immediately assumed.

Had their meeting concluded on time, Ms. Howard would have beat the storm.

He despised lapses in scheduling.

He knew that a difference of an hour could be the difference between life and death.

He had learned that the hard way, long ago and too young, with the death of his parents.

A wasted hour of fuel and you woke up more than half-drowned to the loss of everything you held dear. A wasted hour was enough to make a man wish he were dead, too.

But Benjamin was not dead.

And because of that, he did not waste time.

But somehow, he had with Ms. Howard.

An entire hour had slipped past him unaware while he had been absorbed by the fascinating mind and mannerisms of a woman who was nothing that he expected.

And because of that lapse, she would not be going home tonight.

Because of that, she would spend the first night of Hanukkah with him, rather than whatever else she had planned.

Turning to her, his frustration making his delivery less smooth than it might otherwise have been, he said, "It appears that you *will* be missing the first night of Hanukkah with your family, after all. Feel free to reach out to them via any of the numerous means available. I will have my staff prepare a room for you for the night, and it goes without saying that you will be compensated for your inconvenience."

His assistant turned on her heel at his words, reacting to the situation with her characteristic pragmatism.

Ms. Howard, however, was dealing with the revelation in a different way, her whiskey eyes flashing and narrowing at him.

It was obvious she placed the blame on him.

He shouldn't be surprised. She had shown herself to be an intelligent and quick-thinking woman over and over again through the past three hours.

Three hours…not two.

She was likely recalling the fact that he had been the one to insist she travel to him for the meeting—a meeting that he had arrogantly assured her would last no more than two hours.

Pride had come before his fall. First, they had gone over time, and now a blizzard.

It was enough to crave a drink.

But there would be no silent night of unwinding by the fireplace with something on the rocks tonight.

He had a guest.

"Thank you," Ms. Howard replied thanklessly, her voice flat, before finishing her thought with, "I'm sure my phone will suffice, though. Rather than impose on your family, I'll plan to stay in my room for a quiet night." Her expression turned abruptly serious then. "Really, I'd prefer that. It's been a long day of travel and work and I don't want to be the unexpected guest that impacts your holiday celebrations."

Did he detect a hint of censure in what she said, faint chastisement in the words *travel* and *work*?

He thought he did—because she had spine.

Her use of the word *unexpected* he found interesting too.

The concept clung to her, enveloping her with its many meanings.

The woman, the work, the blizzard—all thoroughly unexpected.

A further example of which was the fact that he had not expected his earlier omission to come back around to him.

Ms. Howard remained under the impression that he had family hidden somewhere in the wings, waiting for him to light candles and hand out gifts and eat doughnuts from LA's newest hot spot.

Now, despite the excuse she had offered him, he would have to correct the misrepresentation.

Once again, Ms. Howard had necessitated a change of his plans.

Rather than correct her impression immediately, however, he said, "We can certainly have that arranged, though it will take a little bit longer before your room is fully stocked and prepared. In the meantime, with work done, we might as well go track down those doughnuts."

Cheering her in the face of the situation was reason enough to manage the memories the doughnuts would stir up.

The question was, would she follow, or would she insist on waiting to hole up in her guest room until the storm passed?

He took his first step, turning to her to with a look in his eyes that challenged her to come along.

Her warm amber eyes flashed.

Of course she would meet his challenge.

Already she had proven she was the kind of woman who met challenges head-on.

She closed the door of the office behind her as she left, the click of the latch engaging echoing around the two of them in the hallway.

The sound signaled that their workday was done, while the silence after it asked *What's next*?

Early as it was, just past 3:00 p.m., the remainder of the afternoon and the long stretch of evening lay ahead of them.

Up until moments ago, they had been colleagues. Now they were a man and a woman alone at his place.

Had these been normal circumstances, he knew exactly what he would suggest they do.

But these were not normal circumstances.

Ms. Howard was not his paramour of the hour, and he typically did not have the forces of nature to thank for a romantic opportunity.

Besides, he didn't entertain in Aspen.

Aspen was his personal retreat, reserved for working creatively and recharging after bouts of making the rounds socially and professionally.

Aspen was for warm fires, and privacy, and building things that had never existed before.

The idea to invite Ms. Howard to meet him here—while he was in the midst of designing a new software project—had only come to him when she had picked up the phone, eagerness to turn the gala around as obvious in her voice as it had been in her emailed correspondence.

She had the kind of goal-oriented energy he appreciated while working and had acted off the cuff, inviting her because he was willing to welcome that energy into his private sanctum.

His impulse had not been wrong.

The three hours he had spent with her had flowed smoothly within the atmosphere he had created in the woods—too smoothly, if the extra hour was any evidence.

Until she had gotten stuck here, of course.

The extension of her visit necessitated a bigger shift than he could have predicted.

"Really," she said again, obviously still thinking of the family he didn't have, "I don't want to impose. There's no need for introductions."

She had gone from no imposition at all to one that was profound, but nowhere near the way she thought or could understand.

Of course, none of it was her fault—and he had been raised to ensure she did not feel as such.

To that end, it was time to clear up her misconceptions.

"You're in luck on that front, Ms. Howard," he said, "as there are no introductions to be made."

"The doughnuts are not with your family?" she asked, offense in her tone.

He chuckled at the censure. "They are not. I believe my assistant planned to distribute them to the staff. Hopefully we are in time to intercept."

He had not intended to reveal his lack of family to her or host her in his home, but circumstances had forced him to shift gears.

Fortunately, he could not have gotten as far as he had in life without learning to pivot.

"Not good enough for the Silvers?" Ms. Howard asked, her eyebrow lifting at the word *staff*, and he realized she still had not yet heard what he was really saying.

Laughing at her pique, he shook his head, before saying more clearly, "Of course not. Benjamin Silver comes from humble beginnings, if you will recall from my legend. Your doughnuts would have been more than acceptable to anyone in my family. I, however, am the only Silver."

Ms. Howard stopped in her tracks at his side. "You're here alone?" She looked not at him as he spoke, but around the two of them, her warm gaze spanning the massive ceilings and exposed beams.

He would have brought a palm to his face if the motion were not likely to irk her even more.

She was still not getting it.

Nor did she appear to approve.

His lips curved up at her expression.

With a small nod, he said, "I am."

"All by yourself in the middle of the woods and snow?" She shuddered lightly on the word *snow*.

Again, he nodded in response to her question,

eyes laughing though he did not let the sound escape. "Not a fan of snow?" he asked.

She shook her head. "I'm not a fan of being cold."

Angling his head at her, he teased her. "Strange. One would think you would dress appropriately for the weather if you didn't like being cold."

Scoffing, she retorted, "I dress for occasions, not weather, and that is because I am a civilized person from a civilized place in which the weather accommodates. I am perfectly dressed for a business meeting."

"Spoken like a true Angelino," he said with a smile, voice warm.

Ms. Howard waved him away with an expressive palm. "That *is* where I live."

His smile faded.

Los Angeles *was* where she lived, and where she should be nearing even now as they spoke, looking forward to enjoying the holiday and sleeping in her own bed.

"The bigger question—" she broke into his thoughts unaware of the direction they had turned "—is what is an Angelino like *yourself* doing out here all alone for the holidays? Shouldn't you be attending or hosting a new glamorous party every night for the next eight nights?"

It was a Hollywood image, and probably even enjoyable, for all that it was nothing like his reality—which she persisted in misunderstanding.

Likely, the concept of family was so secure and immutable that she could not imagine that one could be without it—that the whole of it could be suddenly and violently torn away from you.

He envied her that.

It was not his experience.

But he tried to keep it light with his reply of, "Some people *like* the snow." The words sounded more pinched than he would have liked, but reasonably casual.

Ms. Howard's eyes, however, shot to him with a flash of concern and pity embedded within them.

But then, with a small smile, she surprised him by backing off the subject.

"Figures…" she said, her voice now lit with impersonal humor.

It was too late, though.

He had seen the expression beneath.

Whatever the backstory she had concocted for him, it led her to pitying his lack of family for the holidays.

But there was nothing pitiable about him. And certainly not from her.

Her career was just starting out and struggling while he was firmly established in his field as well as one of the richest men in the world.

How could she possibly pity him?

"Oh, there it is," she exclaimed, her expression of shock distracting him from his thoughts once more.

They had rounded the hallway corner, coming into the open kitchen and informal living area.

Sitting on the shiny marble of his countertop, mirror-reflected against its glossy surface, was the bright teal doughnut box she had brought with her, but the box was not actually what had caught her attention.

Instead, she stared out the wall of windows that revealed the storm that raged outside.

It was a full whiteout, visibility a joke of the past, the snow so dense and wild it looked like a sea that you could look deep into—a churning ocean of wind and ice and snow.

It was otherworldly, like being dropped into the great storm of a foreign planet.

The weather in Colorado was the main event here—a bigger celebrity than any attention-hungry star or man with more money than he knew what to do with.

Like Ms. Howard, it was unexpected and unignorable, and Benjamin appreciated it.

Colorado, and storms like the one that whirled around them, kept him humble. LA tried to make him into a false god.

Ahead of where they stood, offset to the right, a massive fire roared in his oversize fireplace, filling the space with warmth and light that somehow held its own against the raging storm outside.

His assistant would have arranged that it be lit according to his preference.

He liked a nightly fire.

It was the closest substitute that he had yet to find for the comfort of the family he had lost. It might not be able to embrace, but it was alive and warm, as ever-changing as it was steady and dependable.

Stepping out of the hallway and into his private living area, what had seemed luxuriously cozy at first pass was now a scene of power and wonder—the storm outside a primal reminder that even in this day and age, huddling together remained mankind's greatest strength against the forces of nature.

"I've never…" Her words, as much fearful as they were astonished, trailed off, shaking Benjamin from his own regard of the storm.

"I've never seen anything like this," she finished.

And, he noted, taking in the alertness in her body and pallor of her cheeks, she was sensible enough to tremble in the face of it.

He believed in looking unflinchingly at the harsh power of the world around him and demanded the same of the people he allowed in his company. Looking away didn't make things better.

But he didn't want her to be afraid.

In fact, he had the unusual urge to make her feel safe.

Keeping his voice steady and nonchalant, he

gave a light shrug as he said, "I've been through worse out here, but the first one I encountered after coming from LA? It was certainly an experience. And foolish me, back then I did not have the forethought to bring doughnuts."

Her face whipped toward his, her eyes their own form of fire, humor with a trace of relief alive in them.

Lifting a brow, a half smile on her face, she asked, "So which is it, wise forethought or an obvious move to curry favor?" referring to his earlier comments about the doughnuts.

Pleased with the return of her fighting spirit in the face of the storm, he countered with a slow grin, "It can't be both?"

She laughed as if she couldn't help herself, brow crinkling as it came together over her smiling eyes and mouth. Again, he was momentarily stunned, her expression and the sound of her laughter sparks of joy that, like the roaring fire, held their own against the icy storm outside.

Inconveniently, she was more than attractive.

Her spectacular body of curves stacked upon curves—all of them sumptuous and well-formed—was mingled with the flames of her temper and joy that were contained, for the most part, within the bounds of her diligence, intelligence and competence.

It was a knockout combination.

In the face of both derailment and mild terror,

she dazzled him, her eyes alive in the firelight, the whole of her thrumming with vibrancy and heat at least equal to that of the flames.

The attraction that had been a mild irritant throughout their meeting was clearly growing more potent after hours.

Shaking himself, he brushed away the snapshot his mind had taken of her smiling, recalling the fact that he was more than capable of controlling his baser urges for a night.

In making the years-long transition from skinny computer programming major from the California suburbs to one of the richest men in the world, he had both overindulged and learned how to manage his appetite for romantic company.

He knew how, and when, it was appropriate to express interest in a woman, and how to ensure that she liked it when he did, and he used those talents according to the preferences of his life. And his main preference when it came to romantic entanglements was that they not to get too serious.

He had no intention of starting another family that could be lost and made it a policy to be clear about his intentions with the women he got involved with.

Women who were not off-limits to him, as Ms. Howard was—due to both the foundation's non-fraternization policy, as well as the scandal that had led to her hiring in the first place.

"A man who understands nuance," she said,

speaking not to his thoughts, which she could have been, but to his teasing. Referencing another earlier comment of his, she followed with, "I might not be able to go through a box of doughnuts during a two-hour meeting, but I bet I can give it a good go in front of a fireplace after-hours."

"Three hours," he corrected automatically, wondering if she knew that it sounded like she was talking about something else when she said *I can give it a good go in front of a fireplace after-hours.*

Or was only his mind rolling around in the gutter?

Snorting again, she rolled her eyes. "The time's gone either way. The doughnuts, however, are right there," she said, waving a palm toward the bright box on the counter.

And then she was moving toward them and opening the box, helping herself.

He joined her as she chose a pillowy and plump-looking confection, lightly coated with powdered sugar.

He watched her bite into the treat, closing her eyes in delight as she did, and his stomach tightened.

Her entire posture changed in pleasure, softened and eased, and he realized it was not bravado that had driven her to the box but the need for comfort.

Could he blame her? An unexpected and last-minute business trip had been even more unexpectedly extended and now she was trapped with a supervisor she barely knew for the first night of Hanukkah.

Whatever her original plans for the evening had been, he was sure they had been more comfortable than where she found herself.

But like steam rising, a measure of tension evaporated from her form as she chewed.

He wished a bite could be so effective in the face of losing control of a situation for him as it appeared to be for her.

"Mmm…" she hummed, and when she finished, she opened her eyes, the expression in them easier and brighter. "Lives up to the hype, even hours old, abandoned and *obvious*. You should try one." A grin spread across her face as she finished speaking, gesturing toward the open box with her palm. "They're not all jelly, but it seemed appropriate to get a half dozen, tonight being the first night of Hanukkah."

She had meant to encourage him to grab a doughnut, but instead reminded him of so much more: of his family, of almost-forgotten family traditions, of the fact that she was here, isolated with him, as opposed to celebrating the holiday with her own family back at home.

Offering her a smile that did not reach his eyes, he reached for a doughnut, grabbing at random to humor her while his thoughts circled once more around the inconvenience of the storm.

However, as soon as he bit into the fried dough, perfectly prepared with exquisite filling, his mind paused.

It was delicious.

He could remember the last time he had eaten a doughnut.

It had been his last Hanukkah with his adopted parents—the parents who had raised him from early childhood, after his birth parents had left him an orphan the first time.

And of course, by chance, he had grabbed a jelly.

"Delicious," he said, though the flavor was tinged with something bittersweet, before adding, "almost worth the change in plans."

Once again, she snorted. "Speak for yourself. My evening had wine on the docket."

There was humor in her voice, and he appreciated it, but there was also disappointment.

Whatever her evening plans had entailed beyond wine, she was sad to be missing it.

He couldn't replace her loved ones—he knew from personal experience the impossibility of that enterprise—but he had a world-class wine cellar. "Do you like rosé?"

Nodding and smiling, she was nonetheless cautious as she said, "I do."

He smiled. It felt good when he was right about

Ms. Howard. "I've got a Sangiovese dominant, a Tempranillo dominant and a Syrah dominant. All of which would pair well with these." He lifted the bright box.

She considered, a slight frown creasing her brow.

"Melon and floral, meaty, or olive and cherry," he offered.

"Olive and cherry," she responded decidedly.

"Good choice." He gestured to the down-stuffed sofa in front of the roaring fire. "Go, sit," he said. "I'll bring the rest."

An expression he could not read danced across her face before she nodded, and he found himself watching her as she turned to make her way to sit.

Reading people came as naturally to him as reading code or print.

But not with Ms. Howard.

He wondered how long it would take him to get used to the sensation.

CHAPTER FOUR

Miri sank into the sofa, swallowed by its cushioned designer warmth. In front of her blazed the largest in-home fireplace she had ever encountered.

Plush, heated and inviting, the sitting area was a far cry from the hard-lined modern-style particleboard couch she'd purchased secondhand for her own living room, as well as the cracks in the plaster, mostly covered by thrifted artwork, in her 1920s single-story apartment walls.

Mr. Silver joined her with two chilled glasses of delicately pink wine and the box of doughnuts she'd brought.

He had asked her earlier if she normally made it through a box of doughnuts in a meeting.

She had never finished anywhere near to a full box of doughnuts before in her life, but it looked like that might be changing over the next few hours.

Given that this was her first time in a blizzard,

snowed in with a supervisor, she couldn't even find it in herself to feel like she shouldn't.

In fact, given the day that she had had, she couldn't even say doing so would ultimately register as one of the big firsts.

It certainly fell below drinking wine with an astronomically wealthy colleague in front of a fire in his private residence, as well as below being flown out to Aspen in a private jet.

In the face of all of that, what was eating half a box of doughnuts?

She took the glass from him with a "thank you," unsure if she was grateful or not.

While a nice gesture, rosé and delicious doughnuts were still no substitution for her annual night with her friends.

He sat down beside her, placing the doughnuts on the marble-topped table in front of them as he did.

Beneath their feet, a thick sheepskin rug glowed like a bright pearl in the flashing light of the fire, just begging her to curl her toes into its silky softness.

But one had to be barefoot to curl one's toes into a luxurious rug, and Miri still wore her pumps.

Despite the rosé and the doughnuts and the fire and generally opulent coziness surrounding them, there were cracks in the image of winter holiday bliss they presented.

Mainly the lack of bliss or basic familiarity with each other.

Abruptly, her life didn't seem to make any sense anymore.

She sat on a plush sofa alone with a man she barely knew, drinking wine, their bodies angled toward each other.

Finding herself in this position with a man she had only just met was unheard-of for her.

Miri went slow with things, taking her time with love and friendship and anything else that the crush of modern life would let her get away with.

Rushing and being hasty and trusting too soon were things that she had learned the hard way to avoid from the man she had thought she was going to marry.

Her former fiancé had taught her that even three years was not enough time to truly know if someone was trustworthy and steadfast enough to give your heart to.

She had thought it was, but it wasn't.

And she had known Mr. Silver for mere hours.

And yet the alternative to sitting here with him would have been waiting out the storm alone in one of his many guest rooms.

Sometimes circumstances forced unusual behavior.

"Cheers," he said, breaking into her thoughts and jolting her back to the present moment that she had been reflexively denying.

The present was surreally romantic and ideal, a cozy and rom-com-esque situation in which to find herself in the wake of all of the unexpected events that this man had set off in her life over the last twenty-four hours.

"To the gala, and the first night of Hanukkah," he continued his toast, "and the end of this snowstorm, of course."

His glacial eyes had melted somewhat in the light of the fire, warming even further the longer they held hers.

She should have been on her way to West LA to spend the night catching up with the dear friends with whom she didn't get enough time these days.

Instead, she was staring into the eyes of one of the richest men in the world.

She touched the top rim of her glass to his before drawing it back, maintaining his hypnotic gaze as she drank to his words.

The fire crackled, its light dancing across their profiles, and his expression deepened, darkened.

The chilled wine danced across her tongue and her cheeks heated with the sensation, her breath fluttering for a moment at the intensity of him.

Outside the storm raged, powerful enough to make it unclear as to whether or not the sun still hung in the sky. This late in the year, however, the simple time of day—approaching 4:00 p.m.—meant that the star's descent had to be near.

Hanukkah would officially begin soon.

And here she was.

Her experience with Mr. Silver thus far had been surprising and compelling and challenging and stimulating.

She could think of many words that might be used to describe the man in front of her—powerful, attractive, intelligent and demanding came to mind—but she wasn't here to do that.

She was only here because of the gala and because the hand of fate had forced it, not to spend time with Mr. Silver.

"The rosé is fantastic," she said into the silence that had stretched out around them following their toast and first sips.

"Thank you," he said. "I've only recently begun to add them to my collection."

"Rosé not high enough brow for your collection?" she teased, but he smiled.

"On the contrary. You keep forgetting that I don't come from money. There's very little that I'm too highbrow for. I simply had not yet had time to learn about it. I choose my own wines—it makes it that much more personal to drink them."

Miri was glad her skintone kept most people from noticing her blushes.

Anyone who was astute or knew her well would see it right away, but that wasn't most people.

Most people just thought Black people didn't blush.

She didn't think Mr. Silver would be one of them, but they had also just met. He didn't know her.

"It's easy to forget your humble beginnings when you're living out here in the isolated wilderness like only somebody with money would," she teased. "Nothing says old money like minimalism and luxurious isolation."

With a laugh, Mr. Silver gestured around the plush enormity within which they lounged and said, "As you can see, I'm no fan of minimalism…"

"But the isolation," she countered. "*Regular* people prefer to spend their time with loved ones rather than snowy mountains."

But instead of laughter, as she was coming to expect from him in response to pushback, a shadow came to his chill gaze. "And here again, rather than disproving your theory, I am the case in point. I would spend my time with my loved ones lavishly, had I the opportunity. Unfortunately, I do not, as they no longer exist."

"What do you mean they no longer exist?" she asked, something in her resisting the obvious.

He had told her many times now, she realized, in different ways. His mention of being the only Silver, but she had assumed he meant the only Silver in residence. Not the only Silver at all.

"I mean they are dead." He confirmed what was only now dawning on her. "My most recent parents died in a boating accident just after I finished high school."

"And you don't have any siblings?" she asked, barreling on insensitively as if she had lost her mind.

It was just so unbelievable that this incredibly powerful and wealthy man could actually be alone in the world.

Shaking his head, he said, "No. I was a later-in-life adoption for the two of them, raised and doted upon as an only child. Neither of them had siblings of their own and their parents had passed away long before they had even considered adoption."

As fractured and disjointed as her experience of family felt at times, she still had it.

They might not always know where she fit into the family portrait anymore, now that she was grown and branching out on her own, but there remained people to stand beside.

Compassion and sympathy, however, were not what he wanted from her in this moment.

He had told her multiple times now, casually, thrown out as if it did not bother him, and she had not understood.

Now that she had unwittingly pressed him into stating the obvious, he stared at her as if ready to assess her merit based on how she responded to his sad story.

He had not sent her doughnuts on to family as

she had assumed he would because there was no one to eat them.

He was out here alone on Hanukkah not because he chose to keep himself apart, but because there was no one for him to be near.

But he didn't want her pity; she could see that in his eyes, and she even understood it. So she said, "Well, that explains no one else eating the doughnuts."

A small smile cracked the intensity of his expression. "But that means there's more for us," he said, reaching for another. "It's been years since I've had *sufganiyot*," he remarked as he finished the jelly doughnut, eyeing his still faintly powdered fingertips thoughtfully, his expression seeming to hover somewhere between the present moment and memories of long ago.

Each word reverberated through her fire-and-wine-warmed body, while her eyes remained riveted on his expression.

Nostalgia and distant joy mingled in the curve of his wide mouth, and Miri found herself wishing that she had purchased an entire box of jelly doughnuts after all.

Eyes that normally froze her in her tracks looked like a crisp clear summertime sky over the ocean now.

The furrowed brow that so well communicated just how unimpressed it was possible to get lifted and softened now, revealing a character that was as vulnerable as it was masculine and beautiful.

"My mother loved them. She could easily polish off a box over a business meeting." His smile stretched slightly as he spoke, his voice warm and soft and dangerously normal—easy to relax into—and…also beautiful.

"She had no self-control when it came to *sufganiyot*, and she knew it, so she refused to buy them. *Why tempt myself?* She'd ask herself, and us, over and over, more and more times each day as Hanukkah drew near," he continued.

Miri couldn't have stopped her own smile, nor the quiet laugh that accompanied it, if she had wanted to, and she didn't want to.

It was a good story. A happy memory.

"And did you all suffer along with her?" she asked, but he only shook his head.

"Every year on the first night of Hanukkah, my father would pick me up from school and we'd get a box of them on the way home. It became a tradition, the first night of Hanukkah, every year."

Miriam's breath caught in her throat.

She had unwittingly brought him *sufganiyot* for the first night of Hanukkah.

If the unexpected deliciousness of the evening did not, then the kismet of that fact at least made up for her thwarted plans a little.

Her friends would miss her, but they would still have one another.

Mr. Silver would have been entirely alone if not for her and her ridiculous doughnuts.

Her presence mattered more where she was, she realized, than even where she should have been.

Seeming as stuck in the moment as she felt, his eyes caught hers once again.

"The box never made it past that first night at our house, which I would say is a testament to our self-control today," he said, brushing the powdered sugar off his fingertips before reaching for a glazed cruller, his smile turning mischievous and indulgent, perhaps distancing from the vulnerability of his memories. "Then again, though, Hanukkah hasn't even truly begun yet, and we've already broken the seal. We never did that growing up." He bit into the cruller, making a noise of enjoyment that vibrated through Miri with a different kind of frequency than his childhood memories had.

Was his voice the real secret behind his success? she wondered, still feeling the sound of it along the skin of her arms. Did he simply hypnotize people into believing he was a brilliant software designer when really they just liked listening to him talk?

Judging by the wealth on display all around her, she imagined he probably knew what he was doing when it came to software as well, but with that voice of his, it was easy to believe that it was something more supernatural.

Reaching for another doughnut, she was surprised when she leaned back to find him refilling her glass.

Had she finished the first so quickly?

It had gone down so easy, she couldn't recall.

She might have been more concerned about that had his wholesome story not still been playing in her mind—the heartwarming indulgence of it, the togetherness, the normalcy lulling her guard down.

Each detail reached through time, their compulsion even more powerful than the voices inside that cautioned her not to get too comfortable around this powerful man.

She remembered family moments like that, Christmases with the whole group of them crammed together and piled on top of one another—eating, singing, laughing, bickering, sharing love via a myriad of warm gestures and sweets. Easter egg hunts with cousins from across town, birthdays and celebrations, all of that had been not just present but at times overwhelming in her life growing up. Any excuse to gather had been taken, and closeness had been the result.

Her family had been what motivated her to succeed growing up—to make them proud—and what she had looked forward to in order to refresh and recharge her system when succeeding wore her down.

Of course, that had all been before college—

before she had converted, and everyone got awkward about the fact that they tended to gather
around religious holidays.

They continued to love her and would never
think of disowning her, of course; they just didn't
know how to fit her into the picture any longer.

She missed having a place held for herself. She
missed the open, easy feeling of belonging. Thank
goodness for their Fourth of July and Labor Day
barbecue traditions.

She couldn't imagine what it must be like for
Mr. Silver, not merely to have had his relationships strained and altered by time but taken away
altogether.

Taking a decadent bite of Boston cream, she
banished the creeping melancholy and made her
own sound of enjoyment. "That's a really sweet
story. I bet she really loved that you guys did that."

"She complained that we were the reason she
couldn't fit into her old jeans with every bite, but
I think she did. We loved to make her smile like
that, and thankfully, it was easy. Hanukkah was
always her favorite. She was a kid at heart."

Hearing him talk about his mother was making
it harder to hold on to the image of *disapproving
taskmaster* that she had mentally assigned him,
but Miri was high enough on doughnuts and good
wine and sweet stories to not care for the moment.

She could remember who he was, and who she

was, and who he was to her, when she got back to LA.

Tonight, they were the shared parts of something bigger.

And as such, she wanted to break out of the professional box she'd put herself into, too.

"I don't have any sweet family Hanukkah stories like that, but the year of my joining, the group of us got together to celebrate each night of the holiday. We were all still undergrads at this time, before any of us had husbands or kids or careers, so it was easy to spend that much time together. That first year we actually made *sufganiyot* from scratch, with all the oil stains and burns and sticky jelly and sugar you can imagine would be involved in the process. We learned how to cook something different each night of Hanukkah that year. *Sufganiyot*, latkes, brisket, kugel, roast chicken, matzo ball soup…we even made gelt. There were seven of us who joined that year, all undergrads, and a lot of wine that was much, much, much cheaper than this—" she held up her glass "—so it was chaos, but it was also really fun and kicked off our annual tradition. I'm sure none of us could fit into our pants after, either."

In telling the story, Miri realized she hadn't shared it with anyone before. That year had started a tradition and been the seed of what had become her family of friendship.

It was important to her, life path–defining

even, but she had never had anyone to share it with before.

And oddly enough, sitting here drinking wine and eating doughnuts that somebody else had made with the boss she barely knew, no pan full of hot grease or bottle of cheap wine in sight, there was a hint of the same kind of warmth.

As if she were missing it, but not missing out completely.

That could just have been the result of the fire, though.

And the really good wine.

Or maybe it was a Hanukkah miracle, lighting up something inside.

It's just the wine, she assured herself.

It really was amazing wine.

Because it couldn't possibly be the company.

A half smile on his face, he tipped his glass to her. "I'm impressed. I was born a Jew and I've only ever made half of those things."

Snorting, Miri waved the statement away. "You had a mom to cook it all for you. We were all just a bunch of orphans bouncing around together. The blind leading the blind, if not for our fearless mother hen of a rabbi."

"You were all orphans?" he asked, his face more serious than it had been a moment before.

Startled by the shift in him, though she shouldn't have been, given the history that he had shared, Miri said slowly, "Figuratively. None of us came from Jewish families," eyeing him as she did. She knew now why the concept of orphanhood was a literal one for him.

Immediately his posture relaxed, the stiffness that had come to him exiting almost as suddenly as it had entered.

"That's what you had meant by joining," he put together now. "You're a convert."

He said it like it suddenly made sense, and she tried not to take it personally.

Going through any religious or sacred process was not part of the general modern experience of most people—it stood out and she was used to the fact.

Just like she was used to the fact that most people didn't expect a Black woman to be Jewish.

So while she wouldn't have minded if people could have been a little less weird about both, she understood.

Nodding, she said, "I did, early in college."

She braced herself for the typical question that came next: *Why?*

But Mr. Silver instead concluded, "So no sweet family Hanukkah stories because your family is not Jewish, not because you don't have a family. I had wondered when you said that."

The deduction also wasn't what she had expected.

Shaking her head, she confirmed, "No. My family is alive and well and growing by the minute, it seems. My sisters keep having kids and my parents love to have their grandbabies around. I swear their house is louder now than even when we were all little."

"And none of them celebrate Hanukkah with you?" he asked, his opinion on what the answer should be clear in his tone.

Bristling on behalf of her family, Miri replied primly, "None of them are Jewish."

Mr. Silver was unimpressed. "Hanukkah is an easy holiday to celebrate in solidarity. Many non-Jews take part. Kids love it."

Miri snorted. "Not *my* family."

Lifting an eyebrow, he challenged, "Why not your family? Shouldn't your position as a convert make them even more likely to take part?"

Miri had thought so, privately, in the deep recesses of her mind, but she would never say so.

Not to her family, or anyone else.

"They're pretty stuck in their ways, but it's not like they've shunned me or anything like that. We get together regularly, once a month for big family dinners at my parents' house. They still don't really understand my choices, but they support me as best they know how to."

"What's so hard to understand about becoming a Jew?" he asked. "The food is great, and we know how to have a good time."

Miri laughed, saying, "Clearly, I was convinced," even though once again, his question was a penetrating one that she had privately asked herself more than once.

But unlike her family, she had a better understanding of what was going on beneath the surface.

She encountered it a lot more than they did, and because she had transitioned from a non-Jewish to Jewish identity, she had unique insight into the fact that many people thought anti-Semitism had ended with WWII.

Most people, her past self included, had no idea how many of their own ideas of Jewishness fell between incorrect and vaguely uncomfortable to outright anti-Semitic.

Encountering Jewish people directly, born or converts, confronted and agitated those below-the-surface ideas.

Even when there was no doubt they loved you, she reminded herself.

And from her vantage point, able to see what was going on, she could forgive them for it.

She didn't get the impression that Mr. Silver would be so forgiving. He would challenge it directly, every time he encountered it, ice in his veins.

But not, perhaps, his soul.

Because right now, his eyes smiled as he spoke, striking Miri with just how warm and deep they could be. The contrast between them now and their typical icy sharpness made it even seem possible that he burned hotter on the inside.

But that was ridiculous, of course, because he was Benjamin Silver, billionaire software developer.

He wasn't a man whose passions burned.

He was a man cold enough to become rich.

Miri tried to remind herself of that—and to believe it—despite the fact that she was too comfortable with him and enjoying herself too much to give it any backing.

"Well, as evidenced this afternoon with your impressive plans, it is clear you have excellent taste and discernment."

Her cheeks warmed at the compliment, but Miri tried to focus on the work part of it. "Thank you. As much pressure as there is, I'm looking forward to the gala."

Staring at her, his stormy eyes changed once more, deepening and heating even as they conveyed respect. "It will be unlike anything the foundation has done before. People will be talking about it for months to come."

She didn't know if it was the wine or the fire or the compliments, but she was overheating.

She leaned forward to set her glass on the table and stretched her arms upward as she came back, saying, "As long as everything goes according to plan, of course. I might be often right, but occasionally things don't go according to my plans."

Eyeing her with amusement clear in his gaze, he asked, "Such as?"

"Well, let's just see here," she began, listing with her fingers as she dared a cheekiness that she certainly wouldn't have had had they still been in his office. "Going with classic options for the gala dinner, nearly marrying my high-school sweetheart, running away to join the circus and flying out for a brief meeting with Mr. Benjamin Silver are just a few that come to mind," she said, openly naming some of her most disastrous ideas alongside the storm to soften her joking about the fact the she was stuck here when they were both still dealing with the fallout—trusting the part of himself that he had shown her multiple times now, the part with a strong enough sense of humor that he was willing to laugh at himself.

He did not disappoint.

"Yes," he said, mock serious. "It does seem that *some* of your plans go awry. Thankfully, it's only the terrible ones. That dinner, for example…" He trailed off, grinning at her. "At least in that case you had me to lead you back to excellence."

Miri's bark of laughter was natural and loud, even as she rolled her eyes—for a moment entirely forgetting that this was not a close friend she spoke to and instead was Benjamin Silver—her body shaking with mirth. "It's so refreshing to meet a humble rich man," she said, wiping a tear from the corner of her eye.

"We're a rare breed," he said with a glint in his eye that was as seductive as it was humorous.

She couldn't remember the last time she'd laughed like this.

It was hard to believe that *the* Benjamin Silver was the same man who'd just made her laugh so hard she cried.

He was nothing like she had imagined and all the more fascinating because of it.

He certainly made it hard to turn away from him, sable flowing locks and all.

So she didn't. She just watched him. Was there to witness that glint of something more turn sly.

"So, what happened to the high-school sweetheart?" he asked, one corner of his mouth lifting higher than the other, revealing a hint of his sparkling white teeth, and Miri cringed, somehow still smiling.

For the first time in their acquaintance, he asked a common question.

She couldn't blame him, though. It was human nature.

Whenever the subject of her former engagement came up, questions always followed—and she'd been the one to bring it up.

She usually didn't, though.

In fact, the only times she had in the past had been with those she'd wanted to maintain a clear and open slate with.

Mr. Silver seemed to exist in a world with different rules—even the ones she set for herself.

And she couldn't find it in herself to be mad.

Grimacing for effect, she said, "I changed a lot in early college, and after all of that, he said he could no longer envision me as the mother of his children."

She didn't usually feel comfortable sharing these hurts with people, even those she trusted the most.

And here she had with Mr. Silver.

Maybe it was the storm that was changing all the rules?

She didn't know; she just continued, "*Unfortunately*, he realized that in the process of becoming intimate with another woman. They're married and have children now, though, so it seems like he was right."

It no longer hurt like it had—going through the initial emotional agony, there were times when she literally thought she was having a heart attack from the pain of it all—but sitting next to the man at her side, it was nice to realize that time and distance had finally worked their magic.

Just as Mr. Silver's expressive, arresting voice worked its own kind of magic as he lifted his glass and said, inventing a tone that was equal parts sarcastic and sexy as he did, "Congratulations on extricating yourself from a dire situation before it became even more complicated, Ms. Howard.

Things clearly worked out the best for everyone involved in the end."

Surprising herself, Miri laughed again—not as loud or as overwhelmingly as before, but therapeutically none the less.

It was nice to be able to make a joke of it.

That was another one of those things she hadn't been able to do with other people before. Her family and friends had gone through it with her and were too tender to joke about it now.

They felt bad for her and uncomfortable with the details of the story as well as when she mentioned the current life of her former fiancé.

They didn't congratulate her on dodging a bullet.

But she had needed to be free to laugh about it with someone like this.

She realized it in the doing.

She had needed the unusual moments of connection in their conversation as much as Mr. Silver had needed company.

It was something that even her holiday with friends could not have given her.

Laughing lightly, at herself as well as the audacity of the man beside her, Miri said, "At the time I thought the extrication *was* the dire situation, but now I agree."

"So who was this high school Casanova?" he asked, dry and biting and hilarious.

Laughing, Miri said, "A young man I met through youth group."

"Obviously," Mr. Silver nodded, grave, and she hit his shoulder.

She continued. "We met in middle school—"

"Middle school?" he barked, shock clear in his voice, and Miri laughed more. "Is that legal?"

Nodding, she picked back up, "It is. And we didn't go on our first date until high school, and that date was chaperoned by our parents. Our whole relationship happened beneath the watchful and adoring eyes of our parents. Nothing inappropriate." Her chuckling probably weakened the assurance, but she wasn't lying.

"Like I said, lucky to get out before it went too far. It sounds like your fiancé was an idiot. I'm surprised you didn't know it."

Once again Miri's laugh sounded more like a bark, tears sprouting in her eyes at his frank delivery. Shaking her head and wiping at them, she said, "I'm not even sure I quite see how he is now. Weak-willed, maybe. But an *idiot*?"

Mr. Silver shrugged. "He questioned your motherhood potential. I have not known you long, but even after just a short time of working with you, I can tell that you would be an excellent mother. You're dedicated, passionate, innovative, creative, determined, and you know how to hold a line in the face of challenge. Those are the makings of an excellent mother."

She wasn't laughing now, was for a moment instead brought to stunned silence.

She had hurt so much over so many things at that time in her life, but she hadn't realized how much that particular knot had bothered her—not until now, at least, as a virtual stranger massaged it out.

Her cheeks heating, she tried to wave his compliments away. "Like you said. It worked out for the best for everyone."

He nodded. "And even more fortunate, now you don't have to worry about having a stupid man's stupid children. Thank God you practiced good contraception prior to your escape."

Miri gave him a playful punch in the arm. He was terrible.

And yet he had also somehow made an experience that had truly been terrible for her not just bearable, but something she could laugh at.

That might be a Hanukkah miracle.

"Look at you," he insisted, a grin tilting up the corners of his mouth. "You've got an unusually high number of degrees and certifications, an important job at a large foundation, you have a found family of converts, and you're living your best life. Sounds like a happy ending to me." He tipped his glass to her, and she rolled her eyes, looking away so that he could not see her continued blush.

Despite the nighttime glow of the wild snow

outside, there was no longer any doubt as to whether the sun remained in the sky.

Night had fallen in Aspen.

Los Angeles would be only hours behind and her friends would be well into their beloved annual tradition. She had sent messages letting them know what had happened and not to expect her—it had happened occasionally over the years that one of their party might not be able to make it, though this year would be Miri's first time as the absentee.

And there will always be next year, she promised herself.

"They'll be lighting candles soon, I imagine," she said, looking out at the storm only a little wistful.

Next year, she repeated to herself.

"You would have been with them tonight," he said, causing her breath to catch.

Turning away from the window to face him again, the darkness of the storm outside forgotten in the alarm of being understood by this man. How long it would take for her to get used to his level of penetration? He saw and pieced together so much more than the average person.

Nodding her head in the face of the acuity of his mind, she could do nothing but answer honestly, authentic words and feelings spilling out without guard. "I would have. The group of us still meet up for the first night of Hanukkah every year.

Some of us have families now but we still all just pile into the house of whoever has hosting duty for the year and cook together. It's a silly tradition, but I guess I hadn't realized how much I was looking forward to it."

She didn't say any of it angling for an apology, but he said, with all seriousness, "I apologize for my role in the circumstances that have led to your having to miss them this year."

He excelled at what no one else could do—surprising her, and in a good way.

She hadn't needed an apology, and initial frustration aside, she hadn't *really* blamed him—the storm was out of his control—but she appreciated that he understood what she was missing out on and said so.

She wouldn't have thought Benjamin Silver would apologize to anyone—let alone the new hire who had yet to prove herself.

He didn't have to.

But he had, and because of it, her respect for him grew.

"Thank you for saying so. You really don't have to, but I appreciate it." She accepted his apology with the same sincerity that he had delivered it. "Like I said, it's helped me realize how important the tradition is to me and how much my friends mean to me. Those kinds of lessons are what the holidays are all about."

"Spoken like a Hallmark card," he teased with

a light grin, "but true. I can't give you back what you've missed out on this year, but I can promise that you will be taken care of well for the time you are here, Ms. Howard. Anything within my power to provide is yours for the duration."

Given who he was, he had just promised her only about half of the world, and she could see in his eyes that he was serious in the offer.

The restitution mattered to him.

He felt like he owed her, and something in her knew that he was the kind of man who repaid his debts.

And something whispered in her that she might like it.

The power of it sent a strange thrill through her veins.

It was a good thing she wasn't one to use power for evil.

But there was nothing she really needed but to get home as soon as possible and make sure that this gala went off without a hitch, even if, at the moment, the world lay at her fingertips.

"Really, it's fine," she insisted. "It's still just one night in the grand scheme of things, and I can handle the disappointment. And, please, call me Miri." After the scope of their conversation, calling each other by their surnames felt silly and formal.

None of the resolution left his gaze, though his smile took on a warmth that his teasing grin had not had before. "I appreciate your altruism, *Miri*, but I'm not a man used to disappointing. I'm certain there is a way I can make up for it, and when the time comes, it will be done. In the meantime, call me Benjamin." He made her name a sensual experience and followed it with a series of words that rippled through her like an erotic promise—even though she knew he didn't mean them that way.

Despite sharing more with him than she did with most people, at best, the two of them were colleagues in the endeavor of repairing the reputation of an organization they both cared about.

It was impossible that the innuendo she heard in his words could be anything but imaginary.

They both knew what was at stake.

But if someone had told her that she would be on a first-name basis with Benjamin Silver to kick off Hanukkah, she would have responded that *that* would have been a miracle.

If they had said she would be drinking exquisite rosé, reminiscing and making revealing confessions to him, then she would have called security to have them removed.

The idea of it alone was almost as ludicrous as the fact that she could have sworn she saw the same realizations mirrored in his own eyes.

This was *Benjamin Silver*, her project supervisor and one of the richest men in the world.

He was demanding and critical and had no regard for the fact that he had completely disrupted her last twenty-four hours.

He was nowhere near a close friend, let alone a confidant.

He was not someone she could relax around.

And yet here she was.

Eating doughnuts and drinking gorgeous wine in front of a roaring fireplace together.

Relaxing.

Alone in the middle of a storm.

Eyes locked.

Were they breathing in sync with each other?

That would be absurd.

And yet…

The moment stretched longer than it should, longer than two people in a new platonic relationship should stare into each other's eyes in a setting like this, and yet they did not stop.

Emotions that could not be expressed in words skittered across both of their gazes.

It was impossible.

They barely knew each other—had only met in person for the first time that day, had only spoken with each other for the first time within the last twenty-four hours.

He was Benjamin Silver, one of the richest, most sought-after men in the world.

And she was a teetering on the edge of broke forever-student, barely two weeks into a new job.

The current pulsing between them could not be what it seemed.

He couldn't be looking at her like he was promising to make up her thwarted plans to her in an intimate way.

She couldn't be holding her breath in anticipation.

They both knew better.

The lines were drawn in the sand and clear as day.

This couldn't be happening.

So why were they leaning into each other, their gazes drifting toward each other's lips?

Did she make contact first, or did he?

Would she ever know?

Did it matter?

Their lips connected, touched, hers soft and pliant, his wide, strong and full.

One of his hands came to her face, his fingertips tracing the line of her jaw, while he reached around her with the other arm, lifting her chest as he pulled her toward him to clutch her against him, her breasts flaring to life as they pressed into his chest.

With her hand, she gripped his forearm, holding him in their kiss. Her other hand she fisted into the thick silky brown locks that fell to his shoulders.

He growled into their kiss as her fingers tightened in his hair, the sound of his approval egging her on.

Like he had in the office that afternoon, he demanded more from her now—more passion, more access.

As she had earlier, she dug deeper, opened further, and delivered.

His tongue plundered, exploring her, dominant as his mouth made the kind of promises that only full bodies could keep.

Her nipples pebbled against the warm solidity of his chest while she spiraled not out, but *into* him.

Their breath entangled, leaving them both gasping as they angled for deeper connection.

He tasted sweet and heady, like doughnuts and wine, as implacable as the storm outside.

As with work, he wanted her best from this kiss.

Nothing else would he tolerate.

The challenge, spoken in the movement of lips and press of bodies, woke an answering intensity in her.

She would give him above and beyond.

Pouring herself into it, she unleashed all the repressed and unspent sensuality of her past.

It had been over eight years since she'd learned about her ex-fiancé's betrayal and in the interim, while she had been on dates multiple times, she had found it too hard to trust to do anything more physical than offer sweet good-night kisses.

There was nothing sweet about the kiss she gave Benjamin Silver.

Theirs was the kind of kiss that led to more, to hands slipping beneath shirts and needing to slow down, lest inhibitions be forgotten in the heat of the moment.

It was the kind of kiss she hadn't had since the days of being a high-school sweetheart skirting the line of chastity with good intentions and fast-beating hearts.

It rushed, flooded her with heat and reckless-ness that was less concerned with the circum-stances and more concerned with what it would feel like if her skin was touching his.

What would his hands feel like on her breasts? Lower?

She should have been scandalized, a relative innocent clinging to the rational in order to avoid exactly the kind of mess that she had been hired to clean up.

She wasn't.

She was hungry and hot and light-headed on a combination of wine and the sensuality of the man she embraced.

His voice had been seducing her since she'd first answered the phone, his face from the mo-ment she had disembarked the plane, and the hard planes of his body since she'd realized how much rigid strength they held.

He handled her with skill and ease, maneuvering her now as he wanted, running his hands along the curve of her back and down, along her hip, to grip and lift her until he held more of her weight, her very balance in his hands.

He teased her, keeping her teetering on the edge of falling, drowning in the pleasure of his mouth and hands on her body, until she was certain she could take it no more.

Pressing into him, her own hands exploring him through the boundaries of his clothing.

Her fingers found the buttons of his shirt and before she could even register what she was doing, she had begun to unbutton it.

His quiet growls and rasps of pleasure encouraged her, goaded her to continue by virtue of her own power. He was as helpless to her in this moment as she was to him.

Around them, both fire and storm roared and crackled, and yet neither matched the unlocked desire pulsing between the two of them.

Locked up for too long, stirred and repressed and restricted for years, she knew why she was overcome, but why was he?

How was it possible that he could seem as powerless as she was to it?

As his arm once again tightened around her waist, drawing their bodies even closer together, the sounds of the fire and the storm and their chopped and heavy breathing swirled around them like a funnel, only furthering the sense of isolation. Just the two of them existed in the center of this remote universe.

Abruptly, Miri understood what people meant, what her fiancé had meant, when he'd said that he had forgotten about every promise he had made in the heat of the moment.

Feeling Benjamin, tasting him, breathing him in…listening to him…

Oh God… She breathed a sound that was half moan, half sigh into him.

Touching him—the many hard and muscular lines of his body highlighted and accentuated by her hands in a way that his perfectly tailored alpine wear could never hope to achieve—she felt like a teenager again.

And at the same time, like so much more.

The years between now and then, the things she had achieved and the knowledge of self she had gained, shored her up, made her confident and bold in going after what she wanted in a way she had never been back then.

Rather than simply drift away in the pleasure he set off with his lips, she rode the waves, leaning into the swells, an active participant in feeling good.

He let her know he approved by growling into their kiss before bodily rearranging their position, moving her until he had her where he wanted—face-to-face, breast to chest, her knees bent astride him, her skirt hiked past hips to accommodate, core pressed to hot core—refusing to release her lips as he did.

Bringing a hand up to grip the back of her skull, he lifted his hips against her and she saw an explosion of stars behind her closed eyelids.

She gasped and he consumed it, managing her with chiseled control even as she felt the shudders coursing through him through the fabric that separated them.

It didn't matter that they both remained clothed.

She had been naked to him since the moment they'd begun talking.

Since before that, even.

Since he'd told her to do better.

Since he'd seen into her mind through her work and demanded she show him more.

But insightful as he was, she still had depths he'd yet to see, secrets he would have to work much harder for.

She could still do better.

Pressing into him, she wound her hips, slow and deliberate, as much for herself as for him.

She could remind him that he had not had the best of her yet at the same time she drowned in the sensations he elicited in her.

She moaned as he did, his hand tightening in her hair.

Finally, he broke, pulling back for air. Unable to speak, he stared into her wide eyes like he had never kissed a woman before this moment. Like he had had no idea it could feel like this.

A rush of heat flooding her center, Miri could only pant and stare back. She hadn't known.

She had had no idea.

They breathed like high schoolers on the brink of going too far, staring, until he reached for her again, cupping her head gently in his hands to bring them forehead to forehead.

Closing their eyes, they moved in sync, drawing in a deep breath together and releasing it slowly. After another, they opened their eyes again.

"We can't do this, Miri," he said, his smooth voice rough and deep.

In time, she would be humiliated—would reimagine herself sitting astride him wantonly as she was, breathing hard, and be mortified.

She knew that.

But that time wasn't now.

Now she breathed heavy and fought the urge to argue.

Of course they could do this.

They were consenting adults.

No one had the right to tell them they couldn't.

But she *could* get fired.

Creeping hints of the coming humiliation sprouted in the soil of her subconscious.

Leaning back, she brought her palms up to press her face into them.

She was going to get fired in scandal less than two weeks into her job.

Her stomach knotted.

"Miri, I…" Whatever he was going to say was lost as he trailed off.

Rubbing her hands down her face, she started the slow work of disentangling her leg from his lap in the plush sofa, careful to avoid as much contact as possible between her heated, sensitive skin and his body as she went.

I just lost my job.

The thought looped in her mind.

She was straightening her skirt when he reached out to grab her wrist.

The skirt stopped where it was, still hiked up one thigh.

She couldn't avoid his gaze, was once again entrapped in its blue depth.

"Miri. That was absolutely my fault and will absolutely not affect your employment with the foundation."

For the first time in her experience of him, he looked frazzled. His eyes at once imploring—clearly intent on assuaging the most obvious of the concerns that had just sprung up between them—and hot, sparking like blue embers each time they tripped back to her lips or lower.

He didn't want to stop any more than she did,

but he clearly had more sense and self-control in the matter than her.

Her stomach quaked and rolled.

All of the times she had forgotten herself in conversation with him—when she'd let snappiness creep in and when she'd spoken too casually—and now this?

He could only conclude that she was completely out of control—totally unprofessional.

Never mind the fact that derisive judgment was not what burned in his eyes as he watched her.

He wanted her, would have had her, she realized, if she had been someone else, someone whose job wasn't on the line in the having.

She could see it in the way the thrum of his body warred with conscience in his eyes.

They had kissed.

A kiss between single adult coworkers was a far cry from a years-long extramarital affair, but nevertheless, both were against company policy.

He wouldn't tell.

His darkened blue eyes promised that.

He would not threaten her employment with the foundation by revealing what had happened between the two of them here in his remote cabin.

She had to simply trust him on it.

And what was more alarming to her than even the fact that they had crossed the line in the first place, was the fact that she was tempted to do just that.

She couldn't trust herself to be alone around this man if it could get to this point.

For whatever reason, she clearly lacked even basic self-control when it came to him.

And they were snowed in together.

It felt like some kind of cosmic trial.

She needed to get away from him.

Reading her mind, he spoke, his voice thick and raspy. "My assistant will show you to your room, Miri. A good night's sleep and this will be a blip we both eventually forget."

Nodding like making out with strangers on couches was a normal enough thing in her life she could forget about, Miri said, her own voice bearing signs of fading passion, "Thank you."

And when his assistant arrived to take her to her room, after they'd had enough time to gather themselves back to being presentable and fallen into a dense silence in front of the fireplace, she nearly made it into the hall before she turned to say, "Good night, Benjamin."

She shouldn't have used his name—not when the embers between them needed only a little fanning to flame back to life. She should have just gone, girding herself for the incredible awkwardness ahead of them if the storm did not pass by tomorrow morning.

She should have been cold to reinforce the fact that any heat between them was inappropriate.

But she couldn't.

It didn't feel right, not after everything they'd shared—both right and wrong—to leave without saying good-night.

When his voice reached out from behind her, wrapping around her to trail along her arms and leave her shivering in its wake, she somehow wasn't surprised.

"Good night, Miri. Sleep well."

CHAPTER FIVE

BENJAMIN WOKE TO a wall of white and a pounding head.

The wall of white—the storm through his massive bedroom windows—confirmed that, as predicted by the previous night's late weather forecast, it continued unabated.

According to those same predictions, Miri was likely be his guest for at least another day, if not another night.

His pounding head prayed that it would not be another night.

Her kiss was the kind of thing that drove a man to things—and if it wasn't going to be her, which it couldn't be, drink was the only remaining accessible option.

So in the end, he *had* had that hard drink that he'd fantasized about in the afternoon. It had just happened hours later than imagined and after polishing off two bottles of wine with her.

And then he had had a few more after that.

As if he had not already learned this lesson

in college, mixing his alcohols had not been his brightest idea—no matter that each of his selections had been far above top-shelf.

There were some things money could not save you from.

Not many, of course, but some.

A hangover was one if you were as determined to get one as he had been last night.

Sitting up gingerly, he squinted against the bright light drawn in through the wall of windows facing his bed.

Under normal circumstances, there was nothing he liked more than to be greeted by the sun rising over the rolling sea of mountains and trees before him each morning, but normal circumstances for him did not usually include being hungover in the middle of a whiteout.

Storms like this were rare.

As his eyes slowly adjusted to the glare, what had looked like a solid wall of snow transformed into a sea of flurries, with huge snowflakes flying in every direction and visibility of no more than a foot.

As capricious as storms could be, Benjamin did not foresee it lightening anytime soon.

Not only would that mean another day and night with Miri, but likely more still after that.

What was he going to do with her?

As sexy as the images that filled his mind in response were, they were unhelpful.

Kiss or no kiss, those were not the kind of things he could do with Miri.

Last night a combination of drink, nostalgia and confessional had led them into forbidden territory.

Things had gotten out of hand, but certainly not as out of hand as they could have. They had shown restraint.

Admirable restraint, really, when one considered that it was just the two of them here, isolated in the snow far from the watchful eyes of anyone who would ever care or have the authority to do anything about it.

They were a man and a woman with obvious attraction between them and the only barrier was whether or not they could both keep a secret.

Perhaps they had shown *too much* restraint.

The good behavior certainly hadn't made him feel any better the next morning.

It did, however, continue to protect the foundation.

He had to remember that the foundation was what this was all about.

Miri would never have even been to his home to become snowbound were it not for the foundation.

The tiny nonprofit that had coordinated his adoption, a group that did the legwork of connecting Jewish children that fell into the system with Jewish families, had been funded by the foundation.

When he'd reached a place in life in which he had money to give away, he had given it there.

And when he'd reached a place in life in which he had become coveted for boards of directors, he had offered his time to the foundation.

Surely his lifelong gratitude and appreciation for, as well as his now longtime participation with, the group were reason enough to keep his hands, and mouth, off Ms. Howard.

Miri.

His mind corrected the attempt at distancing her immediately; her first name had already become the auto default.

He liked the way it sounded, how it felt in his mouth.

She wasn't Ms. Howard—the new hire he was assigned to work with to salvage the gala. She was Miri—a woman who loved rosé and tasted like vanilla sugar.

He liked her saying his name almost as much.

He felt it as it left her mouth, running along his skin like satin in the silk of her low register, lifting the hairs on his arms as it went.

Each time, it rang through his ears like a preview of what could be, what it might sound like were she gasping it, and paired with the kiss they had shared, left him in a state of mild pain with wanting.

He had intended to give her two hours of his time the day before, no more.

Now they faced days together.

He should be designing software.

Instead, he was mentally rearranging his day to play host.

He had told her he would show her a good time.

He would, and though it was crass, he knew he already had.

A woman didn't respond like she had if she wasn't having a good time.

Now all he had to do was actually deliver on the original intention of his statement when he had told her she would be well taken care of for the duration of her stay, which had not been seduction.

He'd intended to feed her well and keep her company while she was stranded in his home.

He was man enough to provide that, even in the face of their professional breach.

He trusted that they were both mature enough to navigate their morning after, so to speak.

They had to. Both of them would continue their work with the foundation, so they had to.

It would have been easier if he didn't already know what she felt like in his arms.

So he simply would not think about that.

He could not wipe the slate of experience clean—wouldn't want to, in all honesty—but he could certainly set it aside. He was Benjamin Silver.

And he had a guest to feed.

Ringing his assistant through his centralized

intercom system, he confirmed that Ms. Howard did not appear to have woken yet and instructed his assistant to have breakfast prepared for them in the formal dining room.

The long table would remind him to show her the kind of good time that could be discussed over the water cooler.

They could eat and make small talk and Ms. Howard would have a pleasantly impersonal experience for the rest of her time here.

Miri lay in the utter darkness of the room with her eyes wide open, staring up at a ceiling she couldn't see.

She and Benjamin Silver had kissed.

No. That wasn't right.

They hadn't kissed.

They had made out like a couple in the honeymoon phase on his couch in front of a roaring fire.

And then she had slept at his house—not with him, *obviously*, but at his house, and woken up still under his roof.

If she could have taken a walk of shame out of his house to hail a cab home, she would have sneaked out the window without saying goodbye and done just that.

As it was, there was no way out but through him.

And that meant she was trapped forever because there was no way she would ever be able to face him again.

How would she be able to look him in the eye when she had moaned into his mouth the night before?

They had to work together.

Bringing her hands to cover her face in the dark, she muffled a groan.

How could I have made such a stupid mistake?

He was her direct supervisor, the long-standing leader of an organization still recovering from a fraternization scandal.

And she had fraternized with him!

There was no way he could continue to see her as a good fit for her position. He couldn't help but doubt her integrity.

She couldn't help but doubt her integrity—no matter that nothing like this had ever happened before in her life.

Her days of getting hot and heavy on couches were as far behind her as her days of being someone's fiancée.

As a college dater, she'd kept things to the realm of flirting in bars and the occasional good-night kiss at the door.

No man that she had encountered seemed willing to accept the pace she set on intimacy—emotional or physical—so her relationships had a tendency to fizzle out before they got past that point.

She refused to compromise.

She respected herself.

She had set boundaries around trust and a boundary was only as powerful as it was enforced.

Except for, apparently, when she was willing to throw it all out the window.

She had revealed so much and taken things so far with Benjamin the night before that there was no way he could think of her as anything but attention-starved and desperate.

And unless the storm had passed, she was literally stuck with him—no getting out without seeing the judgment in his frosty stare.

Maybe the storm passed overnight?

He was a busy man, busy enough that he'd had only two hours to spare for her and the gala.

He had already gone far over that allotted time, first during their meeting and later, spending hours with her drinking wine and talking.

If the storm *had* passed overnight, then wasn't it entirely possible that he would have to get back to work? That he would have no more time to spare for her and could have his assistant arrange her return to Los Angeles?

A woman could hope.

A woman could also get out of bed, open the curtains, and find out one way or the other.

But if the storm had not passed, getting out of bed would be taking a big step toward facing Ben-

jamin, which was something she honestly wasn't
certain that she could ever do again.

If the storm continued, there would be no escaping the awkwardness of the morning after.

Miri groaned again.

What had she been thinking?

The simple answer was that she had not been
thinking.

She hadn't been thinking about the precarious-
ness of her position, or the importance of the gala,
or the scandal that had been the catalyst for all
of it.

She hadn't been thinking about her boundaries and rules, or being guarded, or holding back
at all—not with the doughnuts, not with the wine
and certainly not with the man.

They had talked about things she didn't talk
about with anyone and done things she had only
ever done with one other person.

Yesterday afternoon they had met for the first
time and by nightfall they were making out on
his couch.

Outside of coeds, who did that kind of thing?

She hadn't even done that kind of thing when
she *was* a coed.

And she had been a coed for almost a decade!

But lying in bed prolonging the inevitable was
not helping her either.

She had to face both what lay outside the window and the man who dwelled inside the winter castle, if she wanted to get home.

And she desperately wanted to get home.

At home she could give herself the dressing-down she deserved for her insane and reckless behavior with Benjamin Silver.

At home, she could settle into the uneasy belief that he wouldn't tell and that she wouldn't tell and that the memory of their little secret would fade into the background until neither remembered it all.

Forgotten, exactly as it should be.

It would be easier to believe in her tiny apartment with a fresh change of clothes on—clothes that didn't still bear traces of his scent from the night before.

Once she got home, she could put it behind her entirely—just as soon as she had a moment to go over every detail of it again, in the privacy of her own space, far away from the man at the center of it all.

She needed both—the examining *and* the forgetting.

And she needed to do it on her own turf, where the ground stayed exactly where it always had— beneath her feet.

And that meant she had to get out of this sumptuous bed and open the curtains.

Bolstering herself, she swung her legs free from

the smoothest sheets she had ever slept in, enjoying the feeling of her toes curling in a plush rug.

Benjamin's home really was comfortable—all the way down to the little details.

When she had first laid eyes on its monstrous size, she had thought there was no way it could be comfortable.

A structure so large would have had to be strange and cavernous, she'd thought, more like an industrial warehouse than a home, but it wasn't so.

He had just made sure that all of the regular elements that made a building a home—windows, rugs, linens, pillows—were oversize and over-the-top to match.

Without a change in clothes, or her sleep bonnet, she had piled her hair up in a high bun and stripped down to her camisole to sleep in. As an option in a pinch, it had worked, but her hair would need some TLC when she got home, and her cami had definitely lost some of its shape through the night.

Maybe if she hadn't spent so much time tossing and turning…

But it was no use grumbling.

Tossing and turning, alternating between wishing they hadn't stopped and wishing they had stopped sooner was the obvious consequence of making out with your boss.

Padding over to the window, she took a deep

breath and then reached out to take the curtain edges in her hands.

Flicking them open in sync with her exhale, she blinked against the sudden brightness in the room, squinting to limit the incoming light.

It was not a bright sun in a blue sky that had her wincing, though.

It was the continued whiteout of the blizzard.

She wouldn't be going home quite yet.

And without the possibility of an impersonal exit, she was going to have to face Benjamin Silver again.

Heat flooded her face and neck.

Pressing cool palms first on her cheeks before moving to her forehead and neck, she sighed.

It was her own fault.

I should have had more self-control, and word-control, and body-control...

There was no point in delaying it further, though.

Her time would be better used putting herself together to face the day, at least as best as she could.

Without her hot-air brush, flat iron or any hair product, there wasn't going to be a lot she could do about her curled and lifted baby hairs and added volume.

Yesterday she had done her usual morning routine and had arrived at the meeting with her normal office look of glossy soft curls—exactly so because she gave herself a mini blowout every morning before leaving the house and didn't skimp on the sheen spray before she used her flat iron to create soft wave curls that framed her face, neck and shoulders.

Taking her clothes into the adjacent bathroom, Miri flipped on the light and took in her sleep-messy bun and lace cami-clad reflection.

She looked like she had spent the night before making out with a man in front of a fireplace.

Her hair was going to require some creativity.

Rummaging through her purse back in the room, she found a few bobby pins and a small tin of cocoa butter she kept on hand to use as a quick moisturizer.

She used the cocoa butter to moisten the soft curling hairs that framed her face before twisting sections in the front back and away from her face, fixing it with the bobby pins just above her ears.

She repeated the process for the other side and smiled at the result in the mirror.

It wasn't the polished shine she normally liked to present at the office, but it was at least appropriate.

She didn't look like she was trying to seduce anyone.

A knock sounded at her door while she took advantage of the bathroom's complimentary toothbrushes.

Jumping, she paused mid-brush to say, "Just a minute."

As she moved, however, a giant dollop of sudsy toothpaste fell out of her mouth and straight down her chin and front, leaving a streak of white froth in its wake.

Fortunately, the disaster had missed her cardigan.

Unfortunately, it had missed neither her camisole nor her button-up blouse.

Double unfortunate was the fact that both were made of silk and would most definitely reveal the disaster—even if she managed to get the white discoloration from the toothpaste out.

"Damn it," she muttered to herself, reaching for a nearby washcloth to dab at the toothpaste residue.

She didn't have time to take it off and rinse it out because there was someone at the door.

Left with long streaks of darkened and wet fabric down her front, she quickly managed to get *most* of the dregs of toothpaste out, but could still make out a faint chalky discoloration through the fabric.

It was the best she could do for now, though.

Rushing to the door, she was slightly out of breath when she opened the door. "Sorry. I was in the bathroom."

On the other side of the door, Benjamin's assistant gave her a flat once-over, but said nothing

to that. "Saw the light beneath the door and figured you were up. Breakfast will be ready soon.
It'll be in the formal dining room, down this hall
and to the left. Think you can make it there on
your own?"

Miri nodded, gifted with a natural sense of direction as well as intimidated by Benjamin's assistant.

A tiny smile cracking her mountain-like face,
the assistant nodded. "Good. Mr. Silver is waiting."

And then she turned on her heel and left.

For a moment, Miri stood in the doorway, staring after her.

And then she forced herself to pull it together
and go out and face the day.

Mr. Silver was waiting.

Benjamin arrived first in the dining room, pleased
at the spread laid out on the table. As pleasurable
as their forbidden kiss had been, the sight before
him was somewhat of a relief.

Breakfast was more akin to what he had meant
when he'd told Miri that he would take care of her.

Growing up in Los Angeles had made him par-
tial to farm-fresh fruit and vegetables, as well as
avocados, and so he had had a state-of-the-art
greenhouse installed on the estate and manned it
with a staff of master gardeners.

Spending as many years in Colorado as he had

now, he also had an appreciation for fresh beef and lamb—and had established an annual contract with a local rancher to buy a guaranteed percentage of his product each year to ensure he had ample supply.

Between those arrangements and the poultry contract he had with a local organic farmer, Benjamin's table was always fresh, vibrant and flavorful—just like he liked it.

This morning was no exception.

Two enormous omelets with fresh goat cheese and basil rested in the large heated dish that was centered between the nearest two end seats of the long wooden table. The table was the focal point of the formal dining room, which, like most of the other rooms in his home, faced enormous picture windows that currently showcased the blizzard.

Around the scramble were platters of fresh fruit, bagels and lox with trimmings, rosemary lamb breakfast sausages, and large mimosas made with orange juice squeezed fresh.

A coffee and tea tray had been rolled out and prepared for them as well, and he was pleased with his staff's presentation.

Regardless of her dietary preferences, she could find something to her liking among the spread.

Rather than sit and wait for her arrival at the table and allowing the moment and his anticipation to build toward the impact of seeing her walk in, he stood beside the fireplace—within which blazed another large fire—and watched the storm outside.

Storms, if not this strong, and well-laid fires were common features of his time spent in Colorado.

Miri was not.

In fact, as the years had gone by, company of any sort—regardless of whether it was here or in California—had become more and more rare.

As he had aged, surrounding himself with people had become less and less effective at disguising the fact that at the end of the day, the only people who cared very deeply about him were shareholders.

People were wrong when they said it was lonely on the top.

It was lonely no matter where one stood if one stood without family.

But here, lost in the woods, loneliness could also be peaceful.

It could be normal.

That did not stop him from turning, though, at the sound of Miri's heels clicking against the hardwood floors.

She wore her clothes from yesterday, of course, but she had changed her hair.

She had pulled it back on either side, revealing cute rounded ears and giving an overall impression of a medieval princess.

She was as striking as she had been the previous day, but softer and sweeter somehow as well.

Or perhaps the softening owed nothing to her clever remixing and everything to do with the fact that he had had her in his arms the night before.

He had clearly spent enough time this morning recalling the more licentious portions of their evening to be struck by her walking through the door.

It was a startling moment when a fantasy became real.

He wanted to touch and taste again what he had already thought too much about.

That was the problem with getting a taste. Once taken, it was hard to pull back.

He wanted to show her a good time again, the way he had last night—not with a lovely brunch but with his hands and mouth.

But today, the second day of not only Hanukkah but of being snowed in together as colleagues, needed to be a reset rather than a repeat.

He needed to keep his hands to himself and his thoughts aboveboard.

He needed to remember he couldn't have her, even while she remained lush and vibrant and entirely entrancing.

"Good morning," he said, smiling with a gesture toward the table. "As delicious as our dinner of doughnuts was, I thought this morning we might have a real meal." He broke the seal on the topic of last night immediately and—he hoped—

softly, in order to lance any potential for discomfort that might exist for her.

Unlike him, she had probably spent her night agonizing not over the fact that they had gone to bed in separate rooms, but because she had fraternized with her supervisor amid the fallout of a fraternization scandal.

He could expect no less.

She was smart and dedicated and clearly determined to keep her job.

He liked the idea of her burning for him more, though, and hoped that perhaps a small portion of her evening had included that.

"Good morning," she replied with a blush and the kind of automatic politeness that told him she'd grown up in an "old-fashioned manners" kind of household. "This looks delicious."

When her eyes fell to the mimosas, though, her voice filled with some of the sarcastic humor he had been introduced to last night.

Lifting a brow, she said, "I see you went with champagne instead of rosé this morning."

Had he been a younger man, he might have said something about hair of the dog, but as she was not aware that he had had anything more than a respectable amount of rosé last night—nor why he might be inclined to do so—he merely smiled smoothly and said, "It complements freshly squeezed orange juice so well."

The look she shot him communicated an eye

roll without any such movement and he was happy they could engage this way following their encounter the previous night.

Some people would be too awkward.

He had known they could both be adults about things, that they could be friendly and cordial and still enjoy each other's company and still maintain a courteous distance.

"Spoken like a typical rich man," she teased, affirming his belief, before adding, "Regular people don't drink fine champagne at every meal."

He gave her a look of mock wounding before smiling and nodding. "It's true. Regular people don't drink fine champagne nearly enough. Have you heard the health benefits?"

She laughed out loud at that, the sound as warm and crackly as the fire, and his smile grew.

This was taking care of her—feeding her and making her laugh.

Not laying her down on the table and eating her like *she* was the meal.

This was what he would provide today.

Casual conversation, rather than confessions—of the private history variety and of the subjects of late-night tossing and turning.

They could make small talk and eat, and perhaps even pass some of the storm time quietly working together again.

She had what she needed from him for the gala, he knew, but his office was equipped so that almost anyone with a white-collar to-do list could work on-site.

And after all of that, hopefully the storm would be abated and he could send her back home knowing that while they may have pushed a few boundaries, there had been nothing more damaging done than a rather tame transgression.

His mind protested the word *tame* in respect to what had transpired between them the night before, but he fought it.

Her body in his hands might have proven to be even more decadent than it had promised to be, but in truth it had simply been a kiss.

One that he would will away if he had to.

Iron will—the kind he relied on to come back to a coding or engineering problem time and again until he had a solution—was the only thing that had stopped him from taking things further with her last night, as the taste of her had made him feel as if he had reverted to being a teenager.

She was responsive and active, full of brilliant heat and warmth, and a part of him would always feel like he had been a fool to let the opportunity to experience her pass him by.

Even if it was an opportunity that should never have arisen in the first place.

Thinking back on it, he could see that the beginning of everything had been bringing her out to Aspen.

He should never have done that.

It was too relaxed here, too at home and comfortable and isolated and natural for anything but actual intimacy.

Intimacy he'd had with Miri.

As soon as she arrived, it had been inevitable.

For his work to be truly creative, he needed an environment in which he could be himself, where he could free his mind and let his ideas roam without limitation.

Only in that space could he come up with the kinds of ideas that could change the world.

His home in Colorado was that place.

Miri's visit—with its losing track of time and honest conversation and passionate embraces—had made it clear, though, that he was *too* comfortable here.

He was too soothed by his fires and sense of home to recall just how big a risk it was inviting anyone into that space.

By necessity, his guard was down here, and without a guard, it was hard to resist Miri.

Which he would do even if she *wasn't* his subordinate at the foundation.

He wasn't looking for the kinds of relationships that the comfort and ease of feeling at home created—which was what Miri's very essence seemed to foster.

He appreciated women—fast-paced women who were not looking to settle down any more than he was—and casual friendships of the mutually beneficial variety that left everyone involved richer for the experience.

Usually, literally.

Unlike Miri, he was not interested in replacing the family he still missed.

As a child, he had lost not one, but two families.

The family of his birth he had lost to a car accident when he'd been just four years old.

Of them, he had only a few vague memories, warm and fuzzy images really, of a man and a woman, and scents that brought them back to mind.

That loss was scarred over and almost unfelt by now.

No, it had been the second time that his family had been stolen from him—fourteen years later when he'd lost his beloved adopted family—that had cauterized any urge in him to try again.

He refused to allow the opportunity for that kind of loss into his life again.

He did not want confidants.

He wanted meaningful work.

He did not need intimacy.

He had his fires.

He wanted to fulfill the promises he had made his parents and enjoy the fruits of his labor in peace.

And to that end, there would be no more inviting colleagues to Aspen.

His compound would return to being solely his

private retreat. Anything else risked the kind of feelings he refused to welcome back into his life.

And yet when he had been alone, after Miri had gone to bed last night, with just the remnants of the doughnut box and her empty rosé glass to remind him that he had spent most of his day with a woman he had only just met—even going so far as to lose track of time with her—it had not been regret that he felt.

Or rather, it *had* been, but not regret that he had brought her into his sanctuary.

It had been regret that he *hadn't* taken her back to his room.

Last night he had been willing to admit that he had enjoyed her company.

Today, however, he would remember the fact that he was not allowed to.

He might be one of the richest men in the world but enjoying Miri's company in any way beyond the brunch they shared now or long planning meetings could get her fired.

And entirely willing to blame the truth of it on Colorado, he already cared enough about her that he couldn't let that happen.

They ate in relative quiet for most of the meal, each enjoying the well-made feast in front of them, with a brief moment in which they each paused to gaze into the incredible storm outside.

"Doesn't seem like it's letting up any," she said quietly, and he shook his head.

"No, it doesn't, and neither is it predicted to anytime soon," he replied.

Moistening her lips, she opened them to say, "It's incredible. So powerful. Able to make it seem like the entire world has disappeared."

She was right, he thought, responding to her words with a nod as he, too, stared at the force outside.

It was easy to imagine the estate was a world of its own—and they the only people in it.

Noticeably shaking herself free from the storm's hypnosis, she gestured to her near-cleared plate. "Everything was delicious. Amazing. Like a restaurant," she said, finishing the last of her plate before leaning back with a champagne glass in her hand. "Thank you," she added.

"I'm glad you enjoyed. I'll pass the word along."

"You have enough staff to cook a meal like this, but I never see them around," she noted, looking around the room that held only the two of them.

The decor of the formal dining room was dominated by natural wood and large beams, and also like the rest of the space, he'd lightened the heavy impression of both by installing massively enlarged windows and utilizing white accents.

He shrugged with a smile. "There's a lot of space and I only hire those who are efficient."

"You like a lot of space, don't you?" she asked, offhandedly thrusting them back into the dangerous territory of personal divulgence.

Did she mean to ask such personal questions?

He doubted it. She was just making conversation.

Of course, making conversation was where things had started yesterday, as well.

"LA sprawls, and yet there is no room," he said, choosing his words carefully so as not to fall into the trap of divulgence. "I'm drawn to the contrast here. A sprawling natural environment in which human spaces are compact. Where they know their place."

"'Know their place,' huh? That's not a loaded statement or anything."

Catching her eyes, he allowed himself a moment to wonder at their whiskey glow before he answered her, "I should say, where humans recall that they are subordinate to the forces and powers of nature. No man, no matter how wealthy or famous or powerful, how loved or cherished, is greater than all this around us." He gestured toward the storm outside and the hundreds of thousands of acres of mountainous forest it hid. "Or really ever in control," he added, appreciating the irony of that embedded in their current situation.

The storm was an exercise in humility.

As well as a reminder that he appreciated as a man with the world constantly at his fingertips.

Lack of control, however. Was a lesson he had been introduced to long ago, with the losses of his adopted family to the sea barely a decade past the loss of his birth family to a flash-flooded road before them.

Death was always a lesson in control.

In Los Angeles, it was too easy to think that a big dream, engineering and money was all that it took to switch things around—to give people the power over nature and life—but it simply wasn't true.

Nothing was ever really in anyone's control.

But Miri was a California girl, through and through.

Had she had a chance to learn that lesson yet?

He watched her face closely for what she might give away without words.

Her response disclosed little.

A half smile gracing her face, she said, "That's actually rather profound. I was expecting it to be more of a 'king of the mountain' thing."

Smiling, he shook his head. "The woman who raised me shudders in her grave at even the idea of that kind of arrogance. Among other things, she was a Bay Area hippie in the sixties. Respect for nature was her jam. I keep having to remind you that I haven't always been one of the richest men in the world."

Lifting an eyebrow, she challenged him. "It's just too impossible to believe that you used to be normal."

Raising his own brow to meet hers, he said, "Just a regular Joe, in every way."

"I doubt that. You have born and bred bougie written all over you."

Enjoying the spark that flashed in her eyes, he said, "If by bougie, you're suggesting I went to good schools, I won't deny it."

She snorted. "I'm suggesting *private* schools and a brand-new car when you turned sixteen. You probably grew up spoiled and don't even realize it."

He laughed but a shadow crept into the sound.

He *had* been spoiled, and even—to some extent—in the ways that she thought.

But mostly he had been spoiled in love and affection.

For which he was grateful.

It wasn't a claim a lot of two-time orphans could make.

But it did make it that much harder to remember the good times.

Some of that shadow crept into his voice, giving it a somber cadence despite his continued smile. "I'm very aware of my blessings," he said, "but my car wasn't brand-new. It was a ten-year-old Subaru my mom only agreed to let me get because of its safety ratings."

At that, Miri let out a bray of laughter, the outburst and volume of it breaking apart his tension at remembering.

"I can't picture you in a Subaru at all!"

"It was a wagon, to make matters worse," he added, enjoying her surprise. "Imagine my sex appeal, showing up to my a.m. coding course skinny and driving a wood-paneled station wagon."

She shook her head holding up a hand, refusing his pitiful image. "Stop! It's too painful."

"Exactly. All-American teen hood, in a single image."

Laughing still, she gestured around her with an open palm. "Congratulations on how far you've come."

Her words echoed his from the night before, when he'd learned about the fiancé that she had narrowly escaped becoming a virtual child bride to, and he appreciated that she could give as good as she took.

She was smart and funny and determined—everything his father had told him to look for in a woman—and it was a strange thing to realize that.

He had thought of his parents—their advice and love—more over the past twenty-four hours with Miri than he had in years.

He wondered why that was.

Was it just because it was Hanukkah, or was it because of her?

He was usually better at keeping the memories, and the associated longing they brought up in him, in the back of his mind.

And yet while they remained bittersweet, something about the way she drew them to the surface was gentle.

Nodding, he agreed. "How far, indeed."

A shift went through her at his words, her eyes narrowing, focusing in on him in a way that set warnings off.

"You miss them a lot, don't you? Your parents," she said.

It did not occur to him to deny it, though he kept his nod short.

Of course he missed them. It would be foolish to claim otherwise, and it was normal to miss lost loved ones, but he was by no means haunted by his loss.

The evidence was all around.

He had not ceased to function, or abandoned his goals, or given up on life.

He had dealt with the pain and picked up the pieces, wiser because he had survived.

He had found a way to be happy again, even through a loneliness that was as impenetrable as the storm.

Everybody was lonely.

He had built a more-than-good life.

"I do," he acknowledged. "The ache has faded over the years, though. And though it doesn't make up for their loss, I *have* had the benefit of not having to explain myself to anyone for the past twenty or so years. But we've digressed. As financially transformative as my story is, it's also boring."

Miri laughed. "Not to those who haven't figured out the formula yet."

"Are you the type to look? I can give it to you for free. It's simple. Hole up wherever you happen to be living for inordinate amounts of time and practice something that can make you rich. Also, have a source of independent financial stability and no one to answer to."

Now she snorted outright. "At least you're honest with yourself," she said, laughing.

"Where else does honesty begin, if not with the self?" he challenged, catching her eye.

Swallowing, a faint blush dusting the apples of her cheeks, she nodded. "So wise. Honesty begins with admitting who we are."

Her voice had gone slightly light and airy, her skin brightening, and he knew she was thinking about last night—and not in agony over it happening but the other kind of agony.

The kind that wished there had been more.

Licking his lips, a thrill lifting his pulse though he maintained a steady hand of control on himself, he said, "And what we want."

Blinking and clearing her throat abruptly, Miri broke the stare first, reaching for her mimosa as she did so.

"It's a good thing we want the same thing," she said, quickly adding, "A good gala, I mean, that is." Stumbling over her words for the first time in his acquaintance, her voice pitchy in its forced lightness, after taking a swig.

CHAPTER SIX

"You wouldn't happen to have a roomful of clothing in every size that rich people always seem to have in the movies, would you?" Miri asked wistfully, aware of the toothpaste stain on her shirt, as they exited the dining room.

"Unfortunately, no. Not here, at least," he said. "At my Palisades home I retain a personal stylist on staff who generally does maintain a wardrobe for guests to choose from, but I don't entertain here."

At his Palisades home... He had a house in the Pacific Palisades?

Pacific Palisades wasn't the wealthiest neighborhood in LA, but it was the most beautiful, in Miri's opinion.

Keeping her reaction to a small choking laughing fit, Miri shook her head.

"It's all right. I'm sure it will pass sometime between now and tomorrow. I can bear another day in old clothes."

As if her words had sparked a memory, he said,

"I can't offer designer attire, but I do have a few less traditional options."

Perking up a bit, Miri said, "Yes?"

"There is a near-endless supply of robes in the spa. I discovered them there on my last use."

Laughing again, at both the idea that he had not known he owned a stockpile of robes as well as the thought of wearing nothing but a fluffy white robe, and said, "No, thank you, though I appreciate the offer. Somehow it feels wrong to wear solely robes through a blizzard…"

Not to mention the fact that the idea of wearing nothing but a spa robe around him set off the kinds of sensations she had been trying to forget about since last night.

Laughter warmed his eyes, his smile remaining, as he said, "Absolutely understandable, and in that case, my second option: I think I have some of my old things from high school that might fit you. It may take some unearthing, but they have a better chance than anything from my current wardrobe. I've filled out since then," he added, a flirty light in his eye that Miri couldn't help but respond to.

"I consider myself generally more filled out than a teenage boy, as well," she said saucily, only partially joking, but his smile only grew.

"You'd be surprised what a height advantage can do to tailoring," he said. "You're a tall woman, but I've still got plenty of inches on you."

She loved being tall and full-figured—had been

praised and lauded for both through her development into a woman—but it often meant she stood eye to eye with the men around her in more than a metaphorical way.

But not with Benjamin.

As he pointed out, he had her by more than six inches.

Focusing in on him now, her attention was drawn to the fact that his height and broad chest were traits she admired in a man.

Not that she spent much time admiring men.

Through a combination of scholastic busyness and her insistence on moving at a snail's pace romantically, dating had happened only sporadically amid her collecting of degrees, moving out on her own and finding a job.

It had just been too hard to get to know someone while juggling all of that, and she refused to be intimate with someone she didn't feel like she knew.

And now that she had a job, she had a gala to save.

She figured she would turn her attention to the awkwardness of modern dating once her career was secure and she had a few years with the foundation under her belt.

At that point her life might have space for the process of coming to trust someone.

But it really didn't now.

And it particularly did not with Benjamin—no matter how much of an ideal height he might be.

He was a man with no time, and she was a woman who required a serious investment of it—once she had some of her own to spare, that was.

As a man, Benjamin was distinctly off-limits.

But wearing his clothes when she needed a change of them was not the same thing as forgetting that.

It was merely a reasonable and pragmatic thing to do under the circumstances.

Facing him with a smile that was probably too big, she said, "If you think they will work. I would certainly appreciate it."

With a nod and a smile that seemed equally forced and overly friendly—as well as an odd mismatch to the heated darkening in his eyes—he gestured in a new direction than they were walking down the hall.

Miri refused to read anything into the look.

You don't have to worry about there being anything more than what's on the surface between the two of you, she assured herself.

They were grown-ups who knew the difference between a heated moment and full-blown attraction.

Today, they weren't anywhere near crossing any lines.

The room was bright and there was literal and

appropriate distance between them—social and professional.

They weren't sitting together in front of a fire drinking wine again.

It was different now.

What had happened was behind them and they could put it out of their minds.

All they had to worry about was when this storm was going to end.

The conviction became harder to hold on to, though, when he led her up some wooden stairs and into an attic where he handed her a forest-green hooded sweatshirt with gold lettering that he had unearthed from the third box he opened.

"From high school spirit week, senior year," he said, his mind clearly in a different place than her own with regard to the sweatshirt. "I swear my mom kept everything," he murmured.

Miri didn't point out that it looked like he had kept everything that his mother had.

Instead, she took the hoodie gingerly, running her fingers along the golden letters sewn onto the breast, proudly declaring the wearer attended California Polytechnic State University.

Only one other time had another man offered her his hoodie, though in fairness, she wasn't sure it was accurate to call her ex-fiancé a man.

He'd barely been nineteen when they'd broken up.

Back then, she had worn his sweatshirt proudly

around town, around the house—around everywhere.

It had quickly become one of her most cherished garments.

Kneading Benjamin's sweatshirt between her fingers, she recalled the texture and familiar thickness of a university pullover, but it wasn't her ex-fiancé's image that came to mind.

Instead, it was Benjamin's, from the night before.

Dragging her mind once again away from the past, Miri responded. "She must have been proud."

Continuing to search through boxes in the climate-controlled attic storage space he had taken her to, he nodded without looking up from what he was doing.

"They were both very proud. Perhaps too proud, ultimately."

The last bit sounded like an afterthought, and yet it carried a heaviness that made it seem ominous to her.

"Their pride was a lot of pressure?" she guessed, unable to stop the part of her that always wanted to take care of everything.

This time, he paused with the boxes, looking up at her as if truly startled out of the task at hand for the first time in their conversation. With a brief shake of his head, he said quietly, "No. Their pride was a wonderful mantle. Unfortunately, it had terrible consequences. They died when the yacht they'd chartered to celebrate my graduation capsized."

Squeezing the sweatshirt to her chest, Miri grimaced. "That's awful. I'm so sorry."

His expression shuttered at her words, and he shrugged. "Bad luck. But it never would have happened if they'd been a little less proud."

"I don't think—" she started to argue, to deny that correlation equated to causation in this case, but seeing his face harden even as she spoke, she realized it was a useless exercise—and probably foolish.

Who was she to know better than him?

She didn't know him.

They weren't friends.

She just worked for him.

And kissed him.

But that didn't make her anything to him or give her the right to push.

"That's a hard way to lose a family."

There was no pity in her words this time, just acknowledgment of the injustice of it.

To lose one's parents in such a horrible accident, and on the eve of college—it wasn't fair, for any young person.

His shoulders relaxed, the line of tension that had stiffened his spine curving back into a natural S.

He smiled at her and it felt like there was respect in that smile.

But had she done the right thing or simply the easy thing by not pushing back against such an obviously erroneous conclusion?

It doesn't matter, she reminded herself.

It wasn't her place to challenge his long-held notions.

He returned to hunting through the boxes for something for her to wear over her legs, and she pushed the question from her mind.

It wasn't her business.

Triumphantly, he held up a pair of sweatpants in the same forest green as the sweatshirt she held.

Between the hoodie and the sweatpants, her attire was going to be a long way from professional, but putting on clothes that didn't have dried toothpaste on them would still feel like a small miracle.

"Thank you," she said. "I appreciate you going to all this trouble," she added, gesturing to the attic and freshly opened boxes.

Closing the box, he rose to his feet with a shrug. "It's the least I could do. I'm sorry I'm not better prepared."

With a dry chuckle, she said, "I'd be worried if you were…"

Turning his neck from one side to the other, stretching out the kinks, he smiled. "I was a wilderness scout, you know… Always prepared."

Miri rolled her eyes, about to say, "Of course

you were," when a box tipped over behind him with a loud clatter.

Miri winced as it landed. It sounded like whatever was in there was both dense and breakable.

The fall dislodged the tape that had held it closed, leaving one flap slightly higher than the other and through the sliver of open container, Miri could make out the green plastic lid of a storage container, but not much else.

"I could have sworn that was stacked securely," Benjamin muttered as he crouched to lift and return it to its place, in the process opening the lid fully to take a quick scan of its contents.

Righting it, he let out a dry chuckle, and said, "Irony of ironies."

Curious, Miri asked, "What's that?"

"It's a box of pictures, including, I'm sure, one of me in the station wagon. And my mom's menorah."

Miri laughed, even as a shiver went up and down her arms. "What are the chances?" she said, and wondered what they actually were.

The random coincidence of that particular box falling over on this particular day—the second night of Hanukkah when they had only this morning been discussing the station wagon—felt a little less random than it should.

"Indeed," he said under his breath as he removed the box of photos. With a remote and oddly robotic efficiency, he sorted through a few photos before handing her one, his eyes still in the box.

In the picture stood a young Benjamin Silver.

Tall and lanky, as he'd claimed, he stood proud beside an old Subaru wagon, wearing the bright and crisp Cal Poly hoodie that she currently held in her hands.

He was obviously himself, and yet it was hard to believe that the man she had spent the past twenty-four hours with was the same person.

It wasn't that he had physically transformed— although as he had said, he had filled out, losing every trace of slenderness in his long body—as much as he had hardened, become more distant and colder.

Especially the eyes.

It was there that he had changed the most.

In the picture, he was a boy, young and clearly eager for the future.

In the present, he was Benjamin Silver, a man with a gaze like an iceberg—chilly, hard and far more intense below the surface.

Had it been losing his parents so young that had done that to him, or was it the ruthlessness required to get as far as he had? Miri wondered.

"There are candles, too. Of course. She was forever worried about running out of candles..." he said, the box containing what she assumed was a menorah in one hand, and unopened box of slender blue and white candles in the other.

Making every move as if he intended to pack it all away, he began to put the candles back into the box, the man he had become was incapable of seeing the magic in the fact that they had stumbled upon a menorah and candles while stranded together on Hanukkah.

But the version of him that stood in the photograph—the same version that was hopeful and bright and went with his dad to get a box of doughnuts for his mom—would have.

He said he wasn't scarred from his loss, but he had just built up so much hard tissue he couldn't feel it anymore.

Surprising herself, Miri said, "Don't put it away. We should take it down with us."

"What?" he asked, looking from her back down to what he held in his hands, as if only now realizing what it was.

"The candles and the menorah. We should take them down," she repeated. "It's Hanukkah."

She tried to keep it casual, sensing that she trod in sensitive territory despite the fact that there was no outward change in him at her suggestion.

"I don't think—" he started, only to trail off for the first time in her acquaintance with him. He picked back up with a shake of his head. "No. No. There's no need for that. This evening is likely your last here and I won't light them after you're gone. There's no need to get wax all over everything and have to clean it up for one night."

Professionalism and basic respect for privacy urged her to leave it at that, but a rogue impulse in her drove her to continue. "I don't mind cleaning up afterward. There's a trick to it I learned during the years that my friends and I were still meeting every night."

She was laying it on thick, reminding him of the event the snowstorm had forced her to miss.

"You're a guest. Guests aren't supposed to clean up."

Miri snorted. "Since when? Everyone is supposed to clean up after themselves."

"Not according to my mother."

"You don't think your mother would be all about lighting those candles?" Miri asked, lifting a brow as she did.

"She also would have fed you a homemade meal for dinner instead of a box of doughnuts. I don't see how any of that's relevant."

"I think we should do it. They fell out of the box, for goodness' sake." She didn't know where the audacity to continue push like this came from, but as usual when it came to Benjamin, Miri could not seem to stem the flow.

"People were burned as witches based on coincidences like those," he said flatly.

Still she didn't give up.

"I don't think we're in any danger of starting a new inquisition."

"It's a waste of time," he said.

"Isn't that what we're looking for as we wait out the storm?"

"Between the room lighting and the fire, you'll barely notice the light of the candles."

"I'd like to, Benjamin," she said, soft and final.

He shut his mouth, pressing it into a straight line. Closing his eyes, he let out a breath, then opened them again. "I'll take them down."

"Fantastic!" She clapped as she said it, warmth blossoming in her chest at the victory, the sensation of it expanding outward like a huge bloom within her, not out of gloating but actual happiness.

It wasn't the battle of wills—hers against his— that she was glad of the outcome.

It was the battle fought inside him, between the hard Benjamin and the open Benjamin.

Angling his wrist to check the time in the hand that held the box of candles, his voice was gruff but had a hint of humor in it—even if it was a self-deprecating kind. "I told them to have dinner prepared at six tonight," he said. "If you want to change and have a little time to yourself and light candles before that, we should head back to the west wing. We'll pass the spa along the way and can grab a robe, in case I'm wrong about the sweats," he added.

Still emboldened after her menorah win, Miri teased, "Not so certain about being right anymore?"

Glancing at her out of the corner of his eye, he shot her a cocky half grin. "It pays to be careful, even if, like you, I am almost never wrong."

It didn't seem like he was talking about the fit of her clothing options anymore, but for the life of her, Miri couldn't pinpoint exactly what it was that he *was* talking about.

He'd assessed her as he'd spoken, eyeing her like she had once again surprised him, but she had no idea why or how.

Leading her on the somewhat long walk back through his home to the west wing, he made small talk about the rooms they passed, including a private theater, a few bowling lanes, both heated and unheated indoor pools, and indoor skating rink.

Along the way, he stopped outside yet another wooden door and went inside, returning with a brilliantly white, gorgeously plush, bathrobe.

For an instant, Miri considered wearing the robe.

The hoodie suddenly seemed thin and rough by comparison.

But as one expected from a robe, its only fastener was the tie at its waist.

A body like Miri's needed far more coverage than that.

Benjamin left her at her room door, something strangely sweet and gentlemanly about the action, before parting with plans to meet up again for dinner in the private dining area, adjacent to the couch and seating area from the night before.

CHAPTER SEVEN

ONCE AGAIN, BENJAMIN ARRIVED before Miri.

Waiting for her for the second time in the same day, he wondered how she had spent the hour or so that they had been apart and considered the fact that a part of him had actually been reluctant to say goodbye to her.

What did that mean?

Despite his commitment to showing her a good time, he had needed the solitude after the incident with the menorah.

It was ridiculous, he knew, to have had such a strong reaction to the idea of bringing it down, but it had surged nonetheless. The last time he had placed candles in the menorah and lit them had been the last year his parents had been alive. There was something visceral in that, a kind of physical memory that could not help but remind him of things that were better off left in the back of his mind.

But to deny Miri's request, a simple and obvious one given the circumstances and time of year—two Jews stranded together over Hanukkah—would be to punish her for the fact that he had things he'd rather remained buried and forgotten.

If it weren't Hanukkah, she wouldn't have even suggested it.

He knew that.

It was a normal, logical idea.

Except that unpacking his old family menorah, freeing all the associated memories it held, wasn't a normal thing for him to do, at all.

And certainly not with a woman he barely knew.

It was an intimate thing to do.

Just like everything else that had occurred between them since their meeting had ended—an hour later than it should have.

For not the first time in his life, what a difference an hour had made.

It was the difference between appreciating the opportunity to work with a woman possessed of a body as fine as her mind and knowing what that woman felt and tasted like.

It was the difference between getting important work done and showing her a good time that was becoming progressively more personal.

He would put a stop to the momentum tomorrow, should the storm continue.

He would create some distance between them,

blaming work if need be, to ensure there were no more slipups.

He had never had to be so diligent around anyone before.

But was it any wonder, really?

Even time worked strangely around Miri, flying by or stretching long in correlation to whether he was deep in conversation with her or anticipating the point at which he would see her again.

It was not an experience he regularly had in his life.

He had mastered time a long time ago.

The death of his adopted parents had been due to losing track of distance and time and running out of fuel in a rickety yacht just waiting to sink, and because of that he had disciplined himself into a man who was strictly aware of each minute as it passed, always knew where he was and insisted on high quality.

He controlled his time, he controlled his relationships, and through that, he limited life's capacity to surprise or hurt him.

But he was frequently surprised when it came to Miri.

At her door, to which he had personally led her through the multiple staircases and long hallways between the attic and her room because he hadn't wanted her to get lost, he had told her, "Dinner will be set for us at the informal table, near the fireplace where we ate the doughnuts."

Heat had come to her cheeks at the reminder of their night, as it had every time anything touched on what they had done on the couch, and she had clutched his old clothing to her chest, her glowing amber eyes racing with thoughts that she did not share. Instead, all she said was, "Great. I think I can make my way back there."

And he had wanted more, had walked away looking forward to the moment when he could have it.

And now he waited for her in the sitting area.

Since when did he wait for people?

He didn't wait for people.

Was there any greater waste of time than waiting for people?

A man could spend his whole life waiting and never get anything.

One had to act, and efficiently, to gain the kind of power and control to impact and save lives.

A man did not get there by waiting.

But, because it was Miri, he was waiting—and because it was her, the wait felt longer than it should have.

While he brooded on the couch and stared into the flames, his staff set the table and quietly left again, abandoning him once more to his private thoughts in his private living room.

"Things took a bit longer than anticipated." Her voice broke into his thoughts first, entirely too welcome. "Turns out this was one of those rare times you were wrong. The high school attire didn't fit and then took me a while to squeeze out of."

Turning in her direction, all thoughts immediately disappeared from his mind.

How was it possible for a woman to look so absolutely stunning wearing a simple spa robe?

The short robe was wrapped and cinched tight around her waist, stretching across her chest at the same time it hugged her hips and skimmed across the tops of her thick thighs, barely covering her gorgeous ass.

On her feet, incongruously and painfully sexy, she wore her work pumps.

Clenching his fists at his sides, he swallowed, his own thighs flexing and releasing as he focused his entire strength and will on not leaping at her.

He had already acknowledged that she was put together like no other woman he had ever encountered.

Now he was forced to admit that he might be developing some kind of kink around it.

At the very least, she had become the prototype for a new fantasy overnight.

"Don't worry about it," he said, forcing himself to be a host instead of a pervert, and she smiled.

The smile was a reward on top of her delicious body, and one that he didn't deserve.

Not when he didn't have the strength to redirect the flow of his thoughts.

"I figured we'd do the candles first," he said, voice rougher than he had intended.

Or perhaps it was as rough as it needed to be, given the fact that she was standing over there looking the way she did when they were about to light candles in his family menorah for the first time since he had lost his family.

There was only so many stimuli a man could take.

"Sounds good to me," she said softly, crossing the space between them, past the set table, to stand beside him in front of the fireplace.

The menorah rested on the mantel, candles in place.

Retrieving a lighter from his pocket, he held it up, gesturing with his other hand for her to do the honors.

Their eyes locked and though he would have thought it impossible only an instant before, for a moment he forgot about even the titillating robe.

Her eyes were so beautiful.

They were warm and boundless, tough and compassionate, brilliant and sexy.

They were the eyes of a woman with good ideas, a welcoming heart, and the strength of will to be honest and real.

They were eyes, he realized, that he couldn't imagine tiring of, even should they be snowbound for the entire duration of Hanukkah.

She moistened her lips, reminding him of what

it had been like to explore her mouth, and reached for the shammash.

He struck the lighter.

To the side of them, the fire in the fireplace made silhouettes of them both, two backlit and shadowed profiles gazing into each other.

She tilted the candle wick into the flame, holding it sure and steady until it caught.

Releasing the lighter, Benjamin watched her, attention focused and detailed, noting everything about her in this moment.

Her hair, the robe, her satin skin glowing in the firelight, her eyes bright—everything about her radiated.

Smiling upon the lighting, she turned to him.

She lifted her chin, angling her face toward his, taking a step toward him—opening her mouth to recite the blessings. It was natural for him to tilt toward her in return.

As if drawn by a force outside of their control, their mouths neared each other—until suddenly she blinked, gave her head a small shake and cleared her throat.

"Maybe it's enough to just light the candles tonight?" she said breathily.

This time she had been the one to come to her senses.

Shaking himself, Benjamin flashed her a sardonic smile before looking up and away, staring into the storm in the darkness outside rather than the woman who was a flame to his moth.

"Certainly," he said, his voice not his own, thick and gruff. "I'm sure you're hungry. The table is ready if you are."

Nodding, she jumped on the subject eagerly. "Yes, starving."

He led her to the table and held out a chair.

She sat delicately, careful to ensure that the short robe continued to cover her ass as she did.

Clenching his hands around the chair, he swallowed as he gently pushed her in.

"Thank you," she said. "Once again, everything looks wonderful. I hope we didn't let it sit too long."

Her voice was airy and light.

"Nothing to worry about. Hot plates," he said, gesturing to the well-set table, each dish sitting on a state-of-the-art warming plate kept at its own perfect temperature.

"It looks delicious," she said, drawing in a deep inhale. "Smells delicious, too."

Recalling her story from the previous night, Benjamin had ordered a slow-cooked matzo ball soup for the night, with sides of grilled fish, roasted vegetables and fresh baked bread.

And once again he had selected the wine for the night, choosing from among the bottles he had the most anticipation around.

The wine was delicious.

The food, however, was unexpectedly disappointing.

Miri didn't think so, however, based on her commentary and sounds of approval.

"It's good," he said, unwilling to disparage his chef in the face of what was arguably a delicious soup, "but something is not quite right."

She laughed at that, the sound blunt and casual and comfortable, and teased, "It's not your mom's."

And though he had stopped being sentimental about his mother's cooking a long time ago—if only because he could no longer remember what it tasted like—he realized that Miri was right.

He had thought he had forgotten it, but tasting the soup tonight, he knew that what was in front of him wasn't it.

Miri, however, leaned back from her plate with a contented sigh. "That was fantastic. It's just too bad we ate all those doughnuts last night."

Laughing that she could crave more doughnuts after their smorgasbord the night before, he said, "No doughnuts tonight. But the chef did put together some delicious blackberry pie and fresh vanilla ice cream. The vanilla comes from my home in Seychelles."

She snorted. "You know they also sell it at the grocery store."

He laughed out loud at that.

There again was that spine, and it was even sexier showing up when she wore nothing but a robe.

"Wait until you taste it before you say that," he challenged, appreciating the way her cheeks shone in the firelight and the aftermath of wine. "I can guarantee you've never put anything in your mouth quite like it."

A familiar duskiness came to her cheeks, a blush darkening them without diminishing any of their glow.

On the surface, he spoke of vanilla but they both knew he suddenly made promises that didn't have anything to do with dessert.

They both understood it, and they were both curious—at least, according to the look in her eyes and the heat of her cheeks.

Watching her, he fought the sense of possession that rose within him.

She was not his, regardless of the fact that she wore his robe and had eaten the food of his world.

Persephone had not been allowed to leave after consuming pomegranate seeds.

They'd had multiple meals now.

Didn't that mean she couldn't leave?

He was surprised to realize he didn't want her to.

Aspen was his private sanctuary, but he was enjoying sharing it with her.

Across from him, Miri cleared her throat, and then shocked him with the words, "So what are we waiting for, then? Time to put your money where your mouth is."

She had to have been aiming for something else, something tough or playfully combative, he guessed—not the provocative challenge that came out.

At least, that was what he surmised by the way her eyes widened after the words left her mouth and her face flamed even further, her plump lips dropping open.

He had kissed those lips only the night before, and she had ended up on his lap when he had.

Could the same happen two nights in a row?

The answer should have been a resounding and absolute no, but it was not.

Instead, he wanted to put the question to the test, to see where she ended up in that little robe.

But he would not act on his impulses.

Things had gone too far last night on impulse. There was no sense in pushing the boundaries for a second night in a row.

Rising, acutely aware of the pulse and throb of each blood vessel in his body, some of which were more insistent than others, Benjamin said smoothly, "If you knew how much I wanted to, Miri."

Words, it seemed, had abandoned him, too.

Whatever he'd been left with had him moving toward something he knew he wasn't supposed to have with unstoppable purpose, careless of all the reasons why he should not.

Turning to get her dessert was the only way he was able to take his eyes off her.

Retrieving their dessert plates from the covered and temperature-controlled containers his staff had left them in, he placed two delicate plates in front of her.

Their eyes locked again, and once again, there was a long moment in which they simply stared.

When she finally said, "Thank you," her voice was rough.

He nodded, replying, "My pleasure," before returning to his seat where his eyes found her again, dropping to the vee where the robe overlapped to cover her breasts.

As tightly as she had initially had it cinched, and it had been enough to bring his attention and appreciation to the way it emphasized the pinch of her waist, it had loosened over the course of their meal, now revealing a tantalizing hint of the swell of her breasts.

He was playing with fire and could not seem to stop.

"Mmm…" she moaned, and his eyes shot back to her face, his body abruptly and absurdly stiff in attention.

It was the ice cream she purred over, not him— her mind far from the prurient thoughts that raced through his head upon hearing the sound—and it didn't matter.

Watching her enjoyment activated his own pleasure.

She savored each bite, balancing warm pie on her spoon with the creamy, smooth ice cream. And each time she closed her eyes, tilting her head faintly back.

She swallowed and he followed the movement of her throat, unable to look away.

Somewhere in the barrage of her indulgence, he managed to finish his own portion, barely tasting it for all that he knew it was delicious.

It did not compare to her.

When she had finished the last bite, she opened her eyes, the whole of her person radiating a satisfied glow. "You were right. That was absolutely delicious."

For an instant, speech evaded him.

Then, clearing his throat again, he said, "I like to deliver on my promises."

Her gaze darkened at his words, her pupils dilating, and she gave her head the tiniest of shakes.

Blushing, she pulled back, energetically as well as physically leaning back, and gave a forced sounding chuckle. "I guess that's how you became Benjamin Silver, self-made billionaire."

He didn't want to talk about how he'd distracted himself from loneliness for years, drowning himself in work in order that he not have time or space to think about all the irreplaceable things he had lost on the boat that day.

He wanted to unwrap the gift that was her robe and appreciate the present inside.

But they weren't supposed to.

It wasn't allowed.

There could be consequences.

She wasn't ready.

Her eyes were wide, and her breath was short, her breasts lifting with each inhale, but she held back.

And he would not push her. Something deep and primal within him knew he didn't really need to.

She wanted to come play with him.

She just seemed to be trying harder to recall why that was a bad idea.

The self-made billionaire Benjamin Silver, as she had called him, knew that sometimes you had to wait to get what you wanted.

"I made my money by having nothing else to live for outside of my calling," he said, joking but also serious. His passion had been the only bridge between his parents and life that existed for him for a long time. "Coding, software engineering, design, all of it came to me as if I had been born with the understanding. It was my parents' greatest wish that the world would recognize that someday. After they were gone, losing myself in my studies and personal projects were the only things I could do to feel like a working part of the planet anymore. By the time I came out of that, I had made my first million. It was easy after that."

He had not planned on being quite so revealing with what he told her, but when had he ever with her? She had a way of drawing more out than he intended to give.

She gave back just as much.

Compassion warred with disbelief in her face. "I don't know if I should be depressed, impressed or incredulous," she said, beautifully honest, as always.

Amused by her frankness, he smiled. "Incredulous," he challenged.

A spark lit in her eyes, and he knew she wouldn't shy away.

"*Easy*? I don't think you know how hard it is out here for some of the rest of us poor souls."

"Of course I do. I told you, I wasn't always rich."

"But you were never poor, either," she challenged.

Lifting an eyebrow, he pushed back. "And you were?"

"Recently, yes," she said, bringing her hands together and closing her eyes as she recalled. "In the gap between graduation and getting the job at the foundation, I was holding it together with piecemeal part-time jobs, but barely. If I hadn't been hired by the foundation when I was, though,

I would have lost my apartment. It was pretty grim there for a while, facing either moving back into my parents' garage or living in my car. But then I got this swanky new job that I must preserve at all costs," she said, smiling with a serious look in her eyes. "I can't afford to lose this job," she added, and in it, he heard unspoken concerns about the security of her position.

There were reasons to dislike being her boss, so to speak. He wanted a different kind of power over her, the kind that ruled body and mind, not paycheck. He resented the shadow of coercion the fact that he could fire her brought into their relationship.

He wanted things to be different between them because he wanted her—even more powerfully than he had their first night together.

And despite that, he focused on her seriously and spoke clearly when he said, "No word will ever come from me that you are not the ideal individual for your position. You've convinced me with your work, and I would never put the foundation at risk of losing you."

Her eyelids fluttered closed, and she exhaled a long breath.

He frowned while her eyes were shut, even more frustrated to have work exist between them.

And yet without the foundation, he would have never met her.

Causing her to fear for her future was not showing her a good time, however. Nor, even, was alleviating that fear.

He wanted to make her smile.

She opened her eyes, expression earnest, to find him staring.

A slight frown drawing her eyebrows together, she said, "Thank you. I was worried after last night…"

"We're fortunate in being hundreds of miles away from anyone who might care, and neither of us is interested in reporting what went down here. As to last night, you have nothing to worry about." It was a promise he would use his considerable power to ensure he kept.

And he would make her smile again.

Voice turning teasing, he prodded her away from the direction of her fears. "So, you've struggled, it sounds like, but only recently. What about in childhood?"

Lifting an eyebrow at his question, she eyed him warily as she shook her head. "As a kid, things were happy and stable. We were never rich or anything, but I didn't have to worry about my needs being met, and my parents were able to afford things that weren't cheap, like piano lessons and judo."

"What did your parents do?" he asked, increasingly curious about everything that made her *her*.

"My dad is a pastor with his own church and my mom works for him as an administrator and all-around helpmate. The congregation pays the bulk of their salaries, which while not crazy by LA standards, was enough for a happy childhood and a bunch of spoiled grandkids."

Lifting his brow in response, Benjamin asked, "A pastor?"

Cringing slightly, Miri nodded. "Yep. There's a reason religious holidays are so big with my family."

A deeper understanding of her feelings of unbelonging dawning on him, Benjamin was softer than he might otherwise have been upon learning the information.

Instead of sarcasm or dry humor, he offered, "I hope he comes around to seeing the great value in interfaith celebrations in the future."

Startled, her face shot to him, her eyes widening as she moved. A look entered them that was part hopeful and part vulnerable, and she swallowed. "Thanks," she said, after licking her lips, and he could tell that as much as she might be afraid to, she hoped that vision would come true, too.

He could tell she missed being a part of moments that were simultaneously familial and sacred.

He was honored to understand that about her. He got the feeling she kept a lot of herself hidden from the world around her.

But she still wasn't smiling.

So he said, egging her on through his tone and arch look, "Judo? I'm intrigued. Piano fits."

Her expression lost a bit of its softness. "And how's that?"

"It's a proper activity for a good Christian girl," he said with a sly grin and a shrug. "But judo? So violent." He shuddered in mock horror and her eyes lit with humor.

"Those of us that went to public school needed to be able to defend ourselves," she teased.

"So you're a public school brat then," he said, pleased to see her lift her chin with a glint coming to her eyes.

"And proud of it," she said, the corners of her mouth finally lifting.

He smiled.

He hadn't had a guess in either direction; he'd simply wanted to see her with her dander up again.

She was beautiful when she sparked.

She was always beautiful.

Blinking to break the spell, he cleared his throat and gestured toward her plate. "Do you want any more?"

She started, confused for a moment as to what he referred to, before looking down at her empty plate. She looked back at him with a smile and a shake of the head. "I couldn't possibly, I'm stuffed. What I want most right now is a comfortable place to stretch out for a post-meal coma."

He chuckled, amused by her way of being frank

without crass, only mildly taken off guard by the satisfaction it gave him to feed her.

Why should providing for her fill him with such warmth? She was his guest, and it wasn't like it was a challenge for him physically or financially. It should have been a basic, second-nature thing to see to his guest's pleasure, and yet the evidence of hers made him pleased and smug—more akin to a caveman providing for his woman than a wealthy contemporary man seeing to his guest's comfort.

The achievement of pleasing Miri felt more like a necessity than a nicety.

"That can easily be arranged. Shall I walk you back to your room and the large bed awaiting you?" he began, only for her to stop him with a quick shake of the head and blush.

"No, no, no. I mean, no thank you. I'm not quite ready for sleep yet," she said, her voice taking on a breathy note it had lacked before. After a swallow, she moistened her lips. "Besides, why go so far when there is that gorgeous sofa and fire just right over there? Plus, the candles haven't burned out…"

Her eyes were like candles themselves, burning bright, their fire searing through everything that covered him.

He swallowed.

They had gone to the couch once before and the results had been…heated.

They'd already been playing with fire—

throughout the entire meal, in fact—and he was struggling to resist the effect she had on him.

"And what if we go too far?" he asked, unwilling to be anything but direct, even in the face of the currents running through his veins.

"No one ever need know if just this once..." she breathed, words thick.

His forearms tensed.

They shouldn't, there were more reasons than one, but they wanted to, and she was right, for the moment, they were the only two people in the world.

"Is that what you want?" He forced the question even as he already knew his answer.

He wanted her more than he could remember ever wanting anything in his life.

But while it could be their secret, it must be the choice of both of them.

There would be no claims of being caught up in the moment, swept away by doughnuts and rosé.

Waiting for her to decide, however, was another torture. Watching her mind work, her silhouette outlined by the fire behind her, his breath bated because of her for the third time that day.

When she nodded, his breath caught, the muscles of his abdomen clenching at the same time.

Picking up the wine that remained in the decanter, he rose, gesturing for her to precede him toward the fire and sitting area.

Her gaze followed the path of his hand, her eyes and mouth widening as they landed on the sofa.

The scene of the crime.

Wise as she was, he knew there was still a chance she might change her mind.

Color came to her cheeks, and she swallowed, the closing and reopening of her lips a sensual thing.

Would her mouth be confident wrapped around him?

With a bodily shudder, he imagined it would.

She looked from the place they had kissed the night before back to him.

Lips remaining slightly parted, breath escaping her, she nodded again.

She stood and again he wanted to groan aloud.

The robe had loosened enough to reveal a hint of the lace brassiere she wore. Her heels clicked across the floor as she walked to the couch.

At the edge of the rug she stopped, and he held his breath, watching her, wondering what she would do next.

His question was answered when she slowly stepped out of the heels, one foot at a time, each one a sensuous rise and fall, before stepping barefoot onto the sheepskin rug and letting out a sigh.

The muscles of his lower abdomen tightened at the sound.

"Everything that happens here, stays here?" she reiterated before taking another step, her question hushed, her voice low and throaty and incendiary—the words heavy with everything they left undescribed. "I don't have to worry about my future with the foundation?"

Nodding though her back faced him, Benjamin did his own swallowing in response, his throat tight from the images her questions sent racing through his mind.

"Yes," he rasped, frozen as he watched her.

At his answer, she did her own nodding.

Without looking back, she moved deliberately then, crossing the rug to sit on the edge of the couch, tucking the short robe beneath her as she did so.

He followed her slowly, trying to rebuild his control along the way.

He had wanted her to smile. He had wanted her to follow him, to take the bait of his invitation to risk returning to the sensual paradise that they had stumbled into the night before.

Now that she had, he was the one who felt like he flirted with danger—like he put something at risk through their encounter rather than her, something far more serious than a new job.

But there was not enough time to think about that in the walk between the table and sofa.

Setting down their glasses and the decanter on the marble-topped coffee table, he poured them each a glass before sitting at her side.

Ignoring the wine, she moved toward him.

It was a small motion, something no one else in the world would record or remember, but he knew he would never forget it.

The reasons why they should not clearly no longer enough to stop her, she reached for him.

Only a fool would not have reached back.

He was not a fool.

Eliminating the distance between them, he gathered her scantily robed figure into his arms, lifting her onto his lap once again as he tilted her face up toward his.

Their lips met, fitting together like puzzle pieces while flames flickered and danced in the fireplace, bathing their bodies with motion-filled light.

Her hands fisted in his hair as their mouths tangled, neither of them reserved or withdrawn.

It might have been snow madness.

It absolutely was.

There had been ample warning.

They were colleagues, not allowed to be lovers.

And yet they came together with smooth and supple ease.

She had moved to him, and then opened like a flower.

He plunged into her, savoring a nectar that was as intoxicating as if it had evolved to attract specifically him.

She sighed into his exploration, pliantly invested, savoring the sensations he brought to her while her fingers gripped his shoulders hard—not, he sensed, in an effort to remain upright, but in order to not let him go. In order that he not stop.

But she was in no danger of him stopping.

He had no stop left in him, save the emergency brakes reserved for her.

Only she could stop him now, not because they shouldn't or couldn't, not because of her job nor his, and not because he wanted to keep her at arm's length.

None of those reasons was more compelling than she was.

None of them greater than his need to have her again—to have more of her.

He did not want a taste followed by another night of tossing and turning, and he was past worrying about it.

He wanted her naked, riding him like he suspected she could, or laid out below him, or presented in front him, on her hands and knees, her curves taking on the shape of the only kind of instrument he was interested in playing.

She looked so damn good in the robe.

It was a shame that it had to go.

Sliding its upper edges over her shoulders while she straddled him on the couch, their position a re-creation of the night before different only in that neither of them seemed to have any intention of slowing things down tonight and there were fewer layers of clothes between them to begin with.

Her beautifully rounded brown shoulders shone soft and smooth in the light, her large breasts looking like some kind of layer cake, dressed in a cornflower-blue lace bra.

Pooling at the base of her gently rounded stomach, accentuating the flare of her hips, moving the robe away had revealed a barely hidden goddess—the kind of woman who was built for everything a man might throw at her.

She had been sexy wearing the robe.

She was out of this world in just lingerie.

Running his hands along her shoulders, he caressed her arms—strong, soft and supple—before cupping her breasts to rub his thumbs along the lace-edge of the half cup. The contrast of her incredible skin against the rough delicacy of the lace sent charged signals up and down his arms but was nothing compared to the jolt he felt every time he crossed over the pebbled treasure of her nipples.

She moaned, her hips rolling on him with each pass, heat pulsing at the center of her.

He had all the money he could dream of, but that meant nothing.

Real power was the capacity to make Miri moan—to bring her to such a state of abandon that she forswore the rules and set them both free.

Unable to stop, he caressed her breasts to the increasing volume of her cries, each one leaving him harder than the last, until he could take it no more, reaching for the fabric belt at her waist.

He made quick work of the knot, flinging the robe away once untied, and beheld the treasure that had lain beneath.

Her panties were lace, the same cornflower blue as her bra, low-cut and stretched across the plane of her abdomen.

Naked but for the faintly transparent blue lace she wore, the reality of Miri surpassed even the fantasies she had already inspired in his mind.

She was shapely and long-limbed, buxom to the perfection of the word, and had miles of beautiful, soft brown skin that begged to be kissed and caressed.

He could have spent an eternity devouring her with his eyes alone, but he did not have an eternity.

He had only until the storm passed to savor her, perhaps only now.

Her head thrown back, eyes closed, as his hands worked their magic, she was everything erotic and sensual he could want. He did not want it to end.

Who knew when they would come to their senses?

If he was half as good as he thought he was, it wouldn't be any time soon.

He would happily drive her out of her mind with pleasure if madness was the only thing keeping reason at bay.

Their bodies pressed together on the couch once more, but tonight it was no longer enough, not for what he wanted to do to her.

Sitting up, he caught her lips again, wrapping an arm around her waist and back, reveling in the press of her skin against his in the process.

Had he ever felt something so soft and begging to be touched?

He had, he realized, but only because he had enjoyed the pleasure of her breasts.

She was the softest material in the known universe, and for better or worse, he knew that now.

Continuing to kiss her, he let his hands slide farther, slipping beneath her thighs to grip her ass as he lifted them both from the couch.

Her arms tightened around him, and she gasped into their kiss but did not break it as he carried her around the marble table to lay her on the sheepskin rug in front of the fire.

He released her lips reluctantly, and even then, only in order to look at her lying beneath him.

He had pictured her like this while he'd been alone in his bed.

Once again, the reality put his mental images to shame.

Her lips were slightly parted, plump and vibrant with their kiss, as sure a sign of her arousal as was the writhing of her body and the roaming exploration of her hands.

He shuddered as she ran the cool silk skin of her

inner thighs along his flanks, her breath catching and sighing at the contrast in their textures—hers smooth and soft whereas he was rough and hard.

The satiny caresses were a glorious preview of what it would feel like to have her legs wrapped around him, but not what he wanted most from her now.

Before that, before he slid inside her and appeased the pressing demand of the beat throbbing low in his abdomen, he wanted to see her free from the frame of her lovely blue lace lingerie.

And before he lost himself inside her, he wanted to taste her, to thrill her, to bring her to the precipice and over, more than once.

He wanted to hear his name on her lips, his first name, husky and thick and desperate. He wanted her to lose herself, to break apart, losing every shred of her incredible control as she did.

He wanted to make sure she never regretted letting the rules that governed them remain outside of the storm, outside of this moment.

Opening her eyes, her amber orbs glowed up at him like bright burning embers in a fire. Her hair was fanned out around her, long and wavy and black, and her lips glistened.

She was phenomenal, and he wanted more.

Leaning down to capture her lips once more, he indulged.

CHAPTER EIGHT

BEING MADE LOVE to by Benjamin Silver was unlike anything Miri had ever imagined, and she'd had years too long to imagine.

And it was nothing like the chaste good-night kisses she had enjoyed throughout college, nor the youthfully exuberant boundary-pushing she had done with her high-school sweetheart.

The passion was there—stronger now even than it had been back then for having had time to ripen and mature—but along with it, there was a level of expertise and finesse that her ex-fiancé had lacked.

Benjamin was superior to every sensual encounter she'd ever had before.

He was intelligent, direct, and knew exactly who he was and what he wanted.

She felt the truth of it with his every exceptional touch.

He was strong and un-shy about what he wanted from her, his confident hands and mouth playing her body like she was an instrument and he a virtuoso.

He had carried her like she weighed nothing, adroitly maneuvering her body into increasingly pleasurable positions.

He knew when to press firm and when to caress lightly, when to command and when to tease, and she was a quivering mess because of it.

Her skin was on fire, even as she shivered across her body. The silken softness of the sheep-skin rug against her exposed skin, the sensuality of his kiss, the pressure of his body pressing against hers, his hips against hers, the rub of his body against her sensitive inner thighs—it over-took her, transporting her out of her body even as it anchored her irrevocably within it.

She was no longer a woman—instead she had deconstructed into a series of sensations.

And yet this was the most womanly she had ever felt.

Like the earth, Miri was hot liquid at her core while the surface of her burst with life and ex-pression.

She sighed and moaned and cried out into Ben-jamin's kiss as his hands trailed along and over her breasts, down her stomach, and lower to gen-tly cup the mound, separated now by only a thin layer of lace.

Deliciously and torturously, he kept his hand

still there, cupping and holding her growing heat while her hips helplessly thrust into his pressure.

Only when she thought she would go crazy from wanting more did he begin to gently undulate his hand, creating slow waves that swallowed her in an ocean of pleasure.

Beneath his expert handling, she writhed, rocking her hips, opening her mouth to his deeper exploration, gasping as he did.

He was relentless as he drove her from pleasure to pleasure, and then his mouth began to travel.

First she felt his lips at the corner of her mouth, then along her jawline, on her neck and her breasts, hot as they engulfed her nipples.

It was too much, and she never wanted him to stop—even as she craved each new thing that came next.

He moved lower, pressing deft kisses against her stomach, giving her no time to process, only time to feel as he tasted and savored her.

When his mouth replaced the hand that had held her core, her thighs clamped around his head of their own volition and she called out his name.

In response, he growled into her, his hands coming to grip her hips and hold her tight.

He ate her through lace, and she burst into a thousand thrumming pieces, her back arching high off the ground while she gripped his hair.

She collapsed back against the silky soft rug

boneless, a half smile on her face while the low rumble of his laugh reverberated through her.

But he was not done with her yet.

Laying a trail of soft kisses along her inner thighs, he pulled up slowly, his movement a gentle caress as she came down.

He rose over her, firm and steady, a smile on his face while his eyes continued to smolder.

Wrapping an arm around her waist, he carefully lifted her, leaning back as he did, until she straddled his seated form with her knees bent while her upper body rested cradled against his chest, held secure and supported by the arm curving around her lower back.

Seated this way, the center of her weighted and stacked atop his, she could easily feel the steel of him through the layers of clothing that still separated them.

He kissed her neck, his hand in her hair angling her head for access, and she moaned.

His hand at her back released the clasp of her bra, sending the straps sliding over her shoulders.

Drawing back slowly, he watched hungrily as the bra fell away to reveal her breasts.

Heat flushed her chest beneath the blue flame of his gaze.

Then, once again, he devoured.

Without the thin barrier of her brassiere between the heat of his mouth and the skin of his breast, she was sure she must be burning.

Heat flared throughout her system again, rising fierce and hot from the embers of her orgasm, and she writhed on his lap while he acquainted himself with her bare breasts.

Until it was no longer enough.

He moved beneath her dexterously, drawing her forward onto her hands and knees now while he knelt in front of her.

She looked up at him, her eyes traveling up his still-clothed form, slowing when they reached the rigid outline of him through his pants before making their way up to his.

He groaned when they did, his hand coming to rake into her hair, cupping the side of her head and gripping for a moment before releasing with an exhale.

"Turn around," he rasped, and she obeyed, though she had never been so exposed to another person before.

He brought his palms to her hips and gripped strong before raking his fingers up to the hemline of her panties to pull them down and over the curve of her ass, feeling as he went.

Abandoning the fabric as soon as he had revealed all of her, his palm once again came to cup her mound. As if she had not already detonated once from the way he touched her, her body wound up again, tensing and thrumming as the movement of his fingers along the edges of her goaded her higher.

Breath abandoned her when his fingers slipped inside of her.

Behind her, he let out a strained moan. "Damn it, Miri, I can't wait anymore. I have to be inside you."

His fingers working steady magic, all she could do was moan and gasp and nod.

Keeping steady hold of her with one hand, his movements took on a new urgency as he freed himself with the other.

The quick clinking of his belt releasing, and the crinkle of the condom wrapper echoed around her, and then she felt him, hot—so incredibly hot— and hard and silken at her entrance.

"Benjamin," she gasped his name, the entirety of her focus zooming in to the place where they touched.

"Be still now, Miri," he commanded, his body poised to plunder yet restrained. "It'd be so easy to slide inside you right now, we both know it, but we're not ready."

Miri tried to listen, tried to behave, and yet still her hips angled back, winding toward greater closeness.

"Naughty Miri," he chastised her softly, his voice low and sexier than she'd ever heard. "I'll forgive you this time, though," he added, guiding her hips where he wanted them with both hands now.

They no longer merely touched, surface to surface, but joined as he pressed into her and held.

"Are you ready, Miri?"

"I'll die if you don't," she choked, and behind her he chuckled low.

And then he was sliding into her and her whole body was shuddering.

He cursed, his voice strained, even as he went slowly, allowing her body time to accommodate him.

It was unlike any sensation she had ever had, stretching, tight, and filling her, even as it somehow made her realize what she had been missing this whole time.

Him.

She had been missing him, this—the perfection of their fit, the strength of him in the core of her.

Moaning, her mind spiraled inward, focused on every way she could feel him, until her inner muscles began pulsing and twitching again.

"Miri," he groaned, his body taut and still as she shuddered around him.

But she couldn't help it; the tide within her rose steadily once again and she could only drift out with it.

And then he began to move, slowly at first, and then with greater speed and depth, until again she dissolved into a million tiny pieces.

And once again, he rocked her steadily through the process of the pieces coming back together, stuttering only when she came back to herself completely on a sigh of, "Benjamin."

His name was both gratitude and awe in her mouth, and as she finished it, his fingers gripped deep into her hips as he thrust one last time before shuddering in the same way.

They remained joined, motionless, while their breath returned, and aftershocks twitched through his body and into hers.

And then he slowly pulled out, allowing her to collapse on the ground and him to lower himself to her side, his eyes swirling as they took her in.

"You're beautiful, Miri," he said as she snuggled into him.

"You're a sex god," she mumbled into his chest as she nuzzled him, mildly aware of the fact that she was naked while he still wore his clothes.

Chuckling again, he said, "You of all people should be clear on the fact that Jews are monotheistic."

Her laughter muffled by their snuggle, she smiled into his chest, filled with a warmth that had nothing to do with the fire and everything to do with feeling free in a way she never had before.

"We should move," he said, adjusting his arm to be more comfortable for her.

Still smiling, she nuzzled in. "No way. I'm not going to my room when you're right here."

Drawing her closer, there was a smile in his voice when he responded. "Of course you're not.

I was talking about my room, where I envisioned we would freshen up before exploring further…"

Even as his words thrilled her, a shadow of apprehension clouded her face. "But just until the storm passes," she said.

His arm tightened around her at her words, though he agreed, "Anything we want, but just until the storm passes."

And for the first time since it had blown in, Miri didn't want it to.

CHAPTER NINE

FOR THE FIRST time in memory, Benjamin was awoken by the buzz of his assistant.

Adjusting so as not to disturb the still-sleeping woman at his side, he pressed the audio-only feed to answer.

"Yes?"

Glancing at the clock as he waited for her response, he was surprised to see that it was 8:00 a.m. He hadn't slept in so late since leaving college.

Of course, it had also been a long time since he'd stayed up so late, and so exuberantly, with a woman.

Within the world of the storm and the safeties of their agreement to suspend the rules of the one outside of it for the time being, Benjamin was happy in a way he had not been in memory.

There was a difference, it seemed, between satisfaction and happiness.

Waking beside Miri made him realize that he had been confusing the rush of the former for the warmth of the latter over his past years and doing so to his own detriment.

Happiness led to sleeping in late.

"It occurred to me that your guest might appreciate a trip to the wardrobe sometime today, since the storm's showing no sign of slowing down. Might be some moths in there with all the use it's gotten since, but Sharice set one up here like she did in California and Ms. Howard might appreciate a change of clothes." His assistant's gravelly voice came through the speaker with even more of its stony quality.

Curled at his side, a naked Miri looked up at him out of one opened eye.

Her eyebrow was lifted and even though she'd only been awake for an instant, there was a *look* in that eye.

"That's an excellent idea, Melba. Thank you. We'll have breakfast in the private dining room today. A repeat of yesterday is fine. I'll wake Ms. Howard."

"Sounds good, sir." And then his assistant was gone, and he was happy to have the world shrunk back down to himself and Miri.

Even with the look.

"You only have spa robes, huh?" she said, head lifted to face him now, both of her eyes open, her hair tousled and gorgeous, a smile beneath the sternness in her tone.

Unable to help himself, he laughed, and it, too, felt as unfamiliar as waking up happy.

"I had no idea. I told you, I never have company out here," he said, smiling. "You're the first."

Abruptly, her sass disappeared, replaced with a warm blush. "Well, today, I will most certainly be making a visit to *the wardrobe*," she said primly.

"And what about ice-skating after that?" he asked. "Or a movie?"

Wariness came into her eyes, even as he could sense her interest. "Are you sure that's a good idea?"

He nodded, sure. He was deliberate when he made a decision. Rarely did he look back once one was made.

"No one knows you're here. No one really even knows we know each other yet. While this storm rages, no one could even take a picture if they wanted to. We've already agreed that whatever happens while you're here will stay here. Why not take advantage and make sure everything happens?" There was an eagerness in his voice, a mischievous enthusiasm and a kind of desperation for her to see his logic that even he could hear.

She turned him into a teenager again.

Once again, she repeated their mantra. "What happens here, stays here."

He resented it, even as it thrilled him.

He was used to convincing his paramours that it was better to be circumspect when dating a man as wealthy as he was but found the fact that it was necessary with Miri distasteful.

He didn't want her to be more concerned with keeping their secret than she was with enjoying it.

"Okay," she said, nodding, her lips lifting into a smile. "But that means candles and Hanukkah, too. At least until the storm passes," she added.

He knew he had clearly gotten the better end of the deal, but he wouldn't be the one to argue.

"Now where did that robe get up to?" she mused, a saucy glint in her eye that he was becoming familiar with.

"Breakfast can wait a bit," he said, grinning, rolling her on top of him all the way.

With the evidence of what he thought it could wait for pressed against her as it was, she only asked, "Again?" with a level of surprise.

Rather than speak, he showed her the answer.

The wardrobe was everything Miri had daydreamed a rich man would have and more. Rather than simply a piece of furniture, as the name suggested, it was a huge walk-in closet—more like a walk-in *room*—filled with outdoor wear, indoor wear, shoes and accessories in a variety of colors, styles and sizes.

"It's stocked for guests, so have your pick and come back if you need to. You remember how to get here?" Benjamin's assistant asked her, after delivering her to what amounted to a private designer mall.

Miri nodded. "I do."

The assistant gave a tiny smile and then made her way out of the room, leaving Miri to make her selections.

It was a shame the storm was keeping them inside, because Benjamin's guest wardrobe had some fantastic coats and snow gear. Passing those options in favor of something more comfortable for indoor wear, though, Miri still felt like a princess.

Who else but a princess had her choice from among high-end designers and cashmere and fine wool? And though she'd been afraid there would be a limit of options in her size, so far, everything she had been drawn to had been in a size that would work for her.

And Benjamin hadn't even known he'd had it.

Snorting, she continued to hunt, humming to herself.

"Don't forget, we're ice-skating today," he said, his voice startling her from the doorway.

She didn't know when he had decided to join her, but it didn't make a difference to her reaction.

Heat filled her at the sight of him.

It was incredible to believe that she had made love to this gorgeous man, with his silken hair and piercing blue eyes, his comfortable, well-fitting slacks and his classy sweatshirt.

Multiple times.

And they would again.

For as long as the storm lasted, and they existed in a world of their own.

One that included fantasy rooms full of free clothes.

"What exactly does one wear to ice-skate?" she asked, tilting her head to one side.

He smiled. "You've never ice-skated?"

Shaking her head, she said, "LA girl."

"There're rinks in LA."

"Not in *my* LA," she said with a grin.

His blue eyes were warm as they watched her, but he answered seriously. "It's chilly in the rink, but still climate controlled. I'd recommend something over the extremities, but you don't need to worry too much about keeping warm."

Taking him at his word, Miri picked out a pair of supple black velvet leggings and a rich creamy oversize amber sweater with a tag that revealed it was 100 percent cashmere.

"What do you think?" she asked, holding them up for his inspection.

Looking at her face, rather than the clothes she held, he said, "Perfect," and her breath caught.

There was no risk of confusing this special time for regular life.

Benjamin Silver was fascinated...with her.

Swallowing, she said, "Fantastic, I'll change into them now."

She turned reluctantly away from him, finding a private alcove in the room to change.

Along the way she found fresh underthings and was again grateful to whomever was responsible for stocking Benjamin's guest quarters.

They had made love again in bed, then again in his shower after that before breakfast, so while her sensitized skin remained alive and quick to fire, she felt clean.

Fresh clothes that cuddled every inch they covered in fabrics she couldn't usually afford almost turned her into a new woman.

She purred at the sensation, and he called from the doorway. "Is that an invitation?"

Flushing all over again, she laughed.

He was insatiable, and she was grateful. She was, too. As she was also acutely aware of how temporary it all had to be.

All of it would blow away with the storm.

The thought was a faint chill in the warmth of the moment, and she pushed it aside, crossing the room to him to take his hand in hers and smile up at him.

Bringing his hand to her chin, he angled her face more openly toward his and took her lips, kissing her deep and lingeringly before pulling back. "It was. You look beautiful and feel even better. The clothes are nice, too."

Eyes closed, she smiled up at him feeling his regard like the sun on her face.

Then she let her lids flutter up and dived into the beautiful blue of his.

"Nice? You're going to have to drag me out of this room kicking and screaming," she teased.

Laughing at that, he easily led her out of the room and down the hallway toward the east wing, where the ice-skating rink lay.

Window after huge window they passed showed that the storm continued on outside as fiercely as it had from the start, and squeezing his hand that held hers, Miri was grateful.

The only fear she felt now in the face of it was that it would end before she was ready.

Benjamin's ice-skating rink was the kind of romantic dream that could have been in a movie. Miri gasped when he opened the door to reveal a room of structured blond wood and massive picture windows, a gray stone fireplace—of course—all surrounding a pristine expanse of ice.

Because the storm continued, all that could be seen through the wall of exterior-faced windows was bright white, but it only highlighted how serene and cozy his private rink was.

The interior wall and ceiling were constructed of long straight planks of the same warm blond wood, almost like a sauna, while the far wall entirely comprised gray stonework with a large floating fireplace at its center.

A seating area was set up in front of the fire, but for the most part, the room was ice rink.

It was all so beautiful that Miri couldn't work herself up about the fact that she'd never ice-skated before in her life.

"Let's get you some skates," he said, almost in response to her thoughts.

"I've never skated," she admitted, even as she still smiled at the room around them,

"I figured when you said you'd never been to a rink," he said with a charming one-sided grin. "Have you ever roller-skated or Rollerbladed?" he asked.

Nodding, she said, "Both, avidly."

"You'll get the hang of it then."

And as she suspected was the case too often, he was right.

Before she knew it, she was evading his capture on the ice, skating and laughing like they were a couple of kids.

"If I catch you, it means I get a kiss," he said as she narrowly escaped him yet again, laughing and breathing hard as she did.

Gliding safely out of his reach, she was cocky. "Tell you what. You catch me, you can have it all. I'm *that* sure you don't have a chance."

Triumph lit his eyes, and she only had an instant to contemplate if she had made a mistake before she was forced to dart away from his grasp as his own skating seemed suddenly in overdrive.

He had not been so fast even moments before, but breathless and laughing as she did her best to elude him, she liked that he had been holding back until he had something worth going full tilt for.

Mere heartbeats later, he caught her, twirling her into the circle of his arms before spinning the both of them around in the center of the rink.

Their eyes remained locked as they spun, saved from dizziness by being each other's anchor—the steady spot to return to.

Their breathing synced even as the momentum of their turn slowed, finally coming to a stop while they stared into each other's eyes.

He held her hand, had taken it sometime in their spinning, and her breasts were pressed against his chest.

Below them, the ground radiated a chill, but she was far from being cold.

But neither did that mean she was ready to strip and lie down on the ice. "You have to take me somewhere warmer to collect your prize," she said, breathless.

"No, I don't," he countered, angling her head to kiss her once more. This time, however, his kiss held notes that had not been there before. Sweet and tender, they gentled his passion. He kissed her this time as if she were a special treasure, something delicate and precious, like ice-skating alone in the world.

She sighed into him, her arms wrapped around

his neck, fire and ice all around them. Her unexpected business trip to Aspen had become a beautiful daydream, even if it was one she would inevitably have to wake up from.

"Thank you for taking me skating for the first time, Benjamin." Her voice was soft and vulnerable because she couldn't help it.

In just under three days, he had become responsible for so many new firsts: her first private flight, her first trip to Aspen, her first meeting with Benjamin Silver, her first blizzard and her first time making love.

And he had made them all luxurious and memorable, fully prepared and equipped to ensure that all her needs were met, even those she had no idea to anticipate.

He was more than equipped to feed and clothe and care for her, with everything at his fingertips in his palatial forest estate—from spare clothing to protection.

Enclosed in the circle of his arms, she was tempted to tell him, but she knew the words would only tangle on their way out. Some things resisted words.

But she was grateful, and she really didn't want it to end.

With their agreements, spoken and not, creating a bubble around them, any reservations that Benjamin had been able to hold on to had quickly dissipated, leaving him with only a sense of urgency to experience Miri in every way he could in the limited time they had.

He had only as long as the storm to build the kind of catalog of images of her that was supposed to last him a lifetime.

He had never resented the foundation before this.

The foundation was the reason he had found Miri—and it was also the reason he could not have her.

With each passing moment in her company, it seemed he wanted her more.

The way she looked up at him, flushed and glowing from skating, however, was an image worth preserving.

As was her laughter as they removed their skates, sitting together on a long cushioned bench.

"You were a competitive figure skater?" she asked incredulously.

He liked her incredulous. He liked her in each iteration he had encountered her, in fact.

"Only until I turned thirteen," he said, smiling in the face of her shock. "My mom grew up in the Midwest, skating all winter, and she wanted that for me, but the culture was different in LA, so instead of hockey, I did death-defying spins."

Miri snorted. "Death-defying?"

"More so than you realize," he said seriously, glad to see her smile grow.

"The rink was part of the reason I chose this property when I came out here," he added. "I missed skating."

Miri nodded, barely holding back her grin. "It's definitely not something that comes up a lot in LA, like golfing."

"Though I'm good at that, too," he said, dead-pan and utterly without humility, and she laughed aloud.

"Of course you are," she said when she could. "And I bet there's a golf course somewhere around here, too."

"You would be correct, though it's only a nine-hole."

She let out the bark of laughter he was so fond of as she set her skates to the side and slid her fuzzy-socked feet back into the fluffy slippers she'd found in the wardrobe.

He couldn't say he wished he had known that his assistant had taken his order to set up his Aspen house the same as his California residence—because he would eternally be grateful for the robe she'd worn to dinner last night—but he was glad to have discovered it existed today, even if just for her excitement in picking out clothes.

He was wealthy enough to be an over-the-top host.

She made it meaningful.

"Only a nine-hole," she muttered, shaking her head, still smiling.

It was remarkable how easy it was to be around her—to talk to her, or not, to make love to her or simply enjoy her company—the only thing it was not easy to do around her was focus on other things, and that was a problem rare enough that he was intrigued.

Work would be there waiting for him when the storm passed.

Miri wouldn't.

So he would go with the way she rerouted the flow, and keep her naked for as much of it as he could.

And, like his past with his parents, he simply wouldn't think about the future.

CHAPTER TEN

"WE'RE COOKING?" MIRI ASKED, staring at the apron that Benjamin had just placed in her still-outstretched hand.

It was the third night of Hanukkah, the second since they'd made love, and they had just finished lighting the candles.

Like the oil and miracle of light, they would be lovers until the storm blew over.

And true to his word, Benjamin had been attentive about lighting them with her this evening—this time they even got through the blessings without devouring each other.

He had been serious when he'd said that until the storm ended, he wanted to experience *everything* with her.

It was phenomenal just how much progress they had already made toward that goal.

This far into the second day of making love to Benjamin Silver, she was even getting used to the fact that her cheeks heated every time she thought of it now.

In the less than twenty-four hours since they'd broken the seal on lovemaking, they'd spent so much time engaged in activities that were erotically sensual that it was a wonder she had not burned completely to ash.

But currently, their Hanukkah candles flickering stoutly on the fireplace mantel, bedroom activities were not on their agenda.

Right now, they were cooking.

"Correct," he affirmed, tying his own apron as he answered her question. "I gave the kitchen staff the night off and ran up and found my old family recipes while you took your post-skating nap," he explained.

He conveniently labeled it a post-skating nap, when in fact, it had been a post-afternoon-lovemaking nap.

He had drawn her from the rink back to his bedroom, where he'd worshipped her with a new kind of tenderness and fervor, going soft and slow and drawing the pleasure out until neither could take it any longer before he drove them both passionately over the edge.

They had fallen together that time, and afterward, he had gently kissed her lips and eyelids before cradling her in his arms like a treasure.

She had fallen asleep warm and safely secure there, listening to the sound of his heartbeat.

And when she'd padded back out to find him

where she expected—the sitting area with a roaring fire burning—he'd handed her an apron.

"We're making latkes!" he added, gathering ingredients now. "And a brisket."

"Your mom's recipe?" she asked as she began to tie her own apron.

She recalled teasing him about it the night before, that only his mother's recipe would satisfy, but he shook his head.

"My grandmother's," he corrected.

Miri rolled her eyes with a snort. "Same difference."

Grinning, he gave in easily with a nod. "Same difference. I'm sure it was her grandmother's before that, too, back in the old country."

It was a common story, to have heritage dating back to the old country, but Miri wondered if he appreciated it.

Growing up, her family Bible held a handwritten record of her family's genealogy—at least her dad's side—but there wasn't much beyond that. They had no wealth of old recipes and photographs to tie them to their history, like Benjamin.

"And what old country is that?" she asked, curious to know the story that had led to him.

Setting her up with onions and a cutting board before he replied, Benjamin began grating potatoes and said, "Ukraine and Eastern Russia. I'm Ashkenazi on all sides, biological and adopted, though my mom, the woman who raised me, I mean, was born in China."

"China?" Miri asked, trying to make sense of it all.

"My adoptive family fled Eastern Europe early, before World War II, going east and eventually making their way to the US through China and San Francisco, as opposed to Ellis Island. Because of that, my mom was born in the Jewish quarter of old Shanghai."

"Fascinating," Miri uttered, placing a wet paper towel on her cutting board to save her eyes from the onion. "And what about your biological family? How do you know about them?"

"Mostly through the adoption agency paperwork and genetic testing," he said. "Unfortunately, on that front I didn't have much to work with. It looks like both of my biological parents' families came the European route, and both came from families hard hit by the Holocaust. It's incredible what havoc an attempted genocide followed by a generation of low fertility can do to a family line."

"I guess it's lucky you even know what you do, then," Miri mused, and he nodded.

"I owe a lot of it to the adoption agency that handled my case," he said. "They focus on making sure Jewish children end up with Jewish families and are meticulous about record keeping along the way. We've lost so much already—they work hard to preserve what's left."

"It clearly made a difference in your life. I'm glad you had people like that looking out for you," she said, and she meant it. The image of a child Benjamin alone in the world filled her heart with sorrow. Instead of falling through the cracks, though, he had had a second chance at a doting family and the support and understanding he'd needed.

For an orphaned child, that was as precious as it was rare.

"Me, too," he agreed. "That's why, years later, when I had reached the point at which I could give back, I chose the foundation. To this day they fund the agency that handled my adoption, and to this day, I fund them."

Despite the fact that the reminder of the foundation cast an unwelcome shadow in her mind, Miri smiled. "Fund it? You run it."

Catching her eye, his filling with the glint she was coming to recognize, he said, "I like to be in control."

Miri shivered, hearing the promise in his words.

She knew from personal experience what it was like to be under his control, and she couldn't say she didn't like it.

Clearing her throat, she refocused on the onions in front of her. "Well, I can see why the foundation is so important to you now," she said, and again, the statement carried a twinge of melancholy.

The foundation was important to both of them,

something far more than just an employer and a position of prestige, and because of that, there was an inevitable expiration to their interlude.

But banishing the dread, if she had to accept that the most sensual and alive experience she'd ever had was doomed to end, she would damn well make sure she enjoyed everything it had to offer along the way.

She wouldn't waste their time being anticipatorily sad.

No, the only crying she would be doing would be because of these damn onions.

Smiling through the welling in her eyes— entirely the onions, she assured herself—she changed the subject with the words, "It's a good thing latkes are delicious, because they're sure a pain in the butt to make."

Two hot and fragrant hours later, they sat at the dining table together again, but this time the meal before them was the result of their own blood, sweat and tears.

Taking it in excitedly, Miri exclaimed, "While I'm sure your chef would have presented it better, all of it looks and smells delicious! I can't wait to eat it."

Benjamin laughed, rumpled for the first time she had ever seen, in the way that only big cooking projects can create. "That's just starvation and hard work talking," he said, grinning at her and their feast.

For the third night in a row, they ate delicious food and drank too much high-quality wine and ended up together on the sofa in front of the fire.

"I could never speak a word against your phenomenal chef," Miri said, a giggle in her voice, "but I have to agree. Your mom's tastes better."

Benjamin tipped his glass to her. "I knew you were a smart woman from the moment I first heard you speak."

Miri's breath caught in her throat.

His mind, his looks, the things he said—he was so arresting. For a moment she could only stare.

In the firelight, his eyes and cheeks glowed with a relaxed ease and warmth that she would have thought impossible the moment she first laid eyes on him.

He was so different, in private like this, from the man who had greeted her on his private tarmac.

That man had been Mr. Benjamin Silver, tech billionaire and board chair of the Los Angeles Jewish Community Foundation—cold and exacting and on a schedule.

Here, though, he was simply Benjamin, no less commanding, but also sensual and easy.

Like lava versus ice.

Hot, he was even more compelling and irresistible than he was chilly.

It felt like so long ago now that she'd even wanted to resist him. It was foolish to resist him—

not because it was hard, but because it was foolish to resist the wonderful and precious gift of feeling close to someone, of inexplicably knowing it was safe to place trust in them, even without having known them long.

It was that very balance of hot and cold that made him worth both opening up to and investing time in. Though he led with cold, the heat within him ensured he would never be devoid of life.

And yet that was the part of himself he kept hidden in the woods.

Tearing her gaze away from him, she looked into the fire and tried to get a hold of herself. The longer they remained in their magical storm, the more theatrical her thoughts became, apparently.

"It's a shame you don't have any family to share the recipes with," she said, trying to find some practical footing again. "They're so delicious and we might be the last people to know it."

At her side, she felt rather than saw him stiffen and turned to him in concern.

Some of the warm openness of his expression had seeped away, leaving something hopeless and grave in its wake.

"If you'd like, I could make you a copy," he offered, not looking at her but staring into the dark storm outside.

She wanted him to smile again.

"Honestly, I'd love that, but family recipes are meant to be enjoyed by descendants, connected people passing flavor and technique and pride down through the ages and all of that. That's what makes them *family* recipes and not just great ones." She'd kept her voice and goading light, to let him know she teased, but if anything, his expression only hardened.

"These are just destined to be great ones, then, because there is no family to carry them on."

"You count as family," she said, wondering if perhaps being adopted had made him feel the imposter, but his next words, his tone sharper than she had yet to hear from him, suggested otherwise.

"Of course I count as family," he snapped, harshness in how fast the words lashed out. "For a moment, I was their new hope for it even. My mom talked about it, how she looked forward to keeping the traditions alive with my kids, how it would keep both her and my dad's families going, blood or no blood." He let out an abrasive laugh. "But that didn't happen. Instead, they died and with them everything else."

"Well, not *everything* else," she said softly. "Not you. And we kept some alive tonight. As long as you're here, it's up to you what lives and dies."

Benjamin scoffed again, his expression dark. "Well, that's a sad state of affairs for them, then, because I'm not going to pass them on."

"Why not?" she asked, gentle, soft, like a deer padding quietly through his deep dark forest.

Turning back to her, anger and hurt in his gaze, lines of his face hard, he gestured around them. "What kind of family could I provide to anyone?" he asked, bitterly. "Resources are not the same thing as a safety net. Four loving parents could not keep me from ending up alone, and there is only one of me. What would happen to any family of mine, should I meet an untimely demise like my parents? It would be irresponsible."

Feeling as if she were stepping through an unexpected minefield, Miri said, "Perhaps that's a burden that wouldn't just fall on your shoulders. Your partner, for example, could provide that safety net."

"Partner?" He sneered at the word. "If the point is to pass on tradition, what is the likelihood that I'll find the *right* partner in my available romantic pool? I'm a billionaire. I don't move in regular circles and most people have something to gain from their association with me. So should I hand my grandmother's recipe to a model that I met at a movie premiere? I can't undo the effects of generations of oppression and trauma by having kids and it's ridiculous to think I could. My mom could have, but not me. It's a losing battle and the possible consequences aren't worth the risk. Fortunately for the world, however, I know my strengths and I've figured out better ways to make an impact than keeping one family's traditions alive."

For a moment, Miri could not think of a thing to say. So much of what he'd spoken sounded more like the logic of pain than the logic of reason, and yet she could hear his conviction—could hear nights and years of coming to such conclusions with no one around to push back.

A part of her thought to argue, but the rest of her suspected that whatever points she made wouldn't matter. Family, the idea of it, the loss of it, was too sore a wound for him.

And one she didn't have the right to prod.

They might be playing at being lovers, but they both knew the game would last only as long as the storm did.

Who was she to suggest that the real reason he didn't want a family was because he had never been able to get over losing the one he'd loved?

Who was she to suggest that he was afraid?

He was Benjamin Silver and she the events director for the JCF.

Finally, she said, "I've never thought of it that way. Not about traditions as part of making the world a better place nor about children as a tool to combat intergenerational trauma. I just love that it feels like you're part of something bigger and more meaningful when you celebrate together and through time, and the idea of introducing new life to how great it can all be makes me happy. You're right about changing the world, though. You've transformed the entire world, Benjamin. In a way you're already going to live forever, but sometimes it seems like you're afraid to be alive."

He stared at her quietly, his eyes burning with intense blue fire, his face as hard as it'd been before she'd opened her mouth, and yet inside, she got the sense that he was on the edge of shattering.

After what felt like an eternity, he blinked, then closed his eyes, bringing a hand up to pinch the space between his eyebrows. Then he let out a long exhale.

Then he looked back at her, and his eyes were wide open again and because of that, she could see that deep inside him was an agonizing mixture of grief and pain.

He sounded older, his voice faded in places, when he said, "I'm afraid to lose everything I love again."

His words reached through the space between them and into her—as if they were true for her as well.

Maybe they were?

Hadn't she kept men at arm's length since being hurt as a young woman? Didn't she ache for the familial ease she'd had before she had discovered who she was?

She realized now that she had kept herself from a great deal of enjoyment and connection because of that very fear.

He had shown her that, even if he struggled to access it himself.

And there was nothing she could do to reassure him.

Her words, triggering though they clearly could be, could not convince him that he was wrong in assuming the worst for all outcomes.

And even if she wanted to, she could not be the one to show him that there were plenty of women in the world who were strong and true enough to help him carry traditions forward. The constraints built into their relationship ensured that she could not, guaranteed that everything between them would disappear with the storm—like Cinderella's magic dissolving at midnight.

She couldn't tease him, as much as the idea brought a sour taste to her mouth, that some of those women might even be models he met at a premiere.

How she wished she could, though—not tease him or convince him to believe in possibilities, but to be the one to prove them to him.

But that wasn't a role for her because she already had an assigned place in his life.

She was the events director of the foundation he was involved with. As much as she was coming to hate it, the truth was that everything between them was predicated on that being the primary and most important role in her life.

A few days ago, she couldn't have fathomed wanting it to be any other way.

What a difference a few days could make.

The difference between that and wishing there could have been room in her life to play a different role for him, a more important and permanent one.

She'd stumbled into facing her own fears with him over the past few days, but it had required a blizzard, unbelievable circumstances, and a lot of high-dollar wine.

She couldn't give him those things—he already had them.

She could only give him what she had right now—herself.

She could give him something to remember.

Gently she placed her palms on his shoulders and pressed him back against the couch.

Eyes still locked on hers, he allowed her to push him back until he met the plush arm.

Miri leaned forward to press a soft kiss to his lips and his eyes closed, head angling to give her access.

She touched him softly, featherlight and sweet, knowing he needed more of that in his life, but she remained in control, pressing kisses to his lips and temples, luring and teasing him into opening up and following him.

And he did.

He had admitted his deep truth to her and now he let her tend to it, let her comfort and lull him though he so feared letting his guard down.

She kissed down his neck, pressing her lips

even against the soft, thin fabric of his sweater as she traveled south.

Breath escaped him when she came to his belt.

Lifting the hem of his clothing, she exposed the skin of his lower abdomen and kissed there, too, a jolt of electricity jumping between them as she did.

Inhaling him, she removed his belt and exposed even more of him to the firelight.

Then she took him in her mouth and showed him that—at least while he was with her in this storm—it was okay to be afraid.

CHAPTER ELEVEN

THAT IT WAS now the sixth day of Hanukkah and still the storm continued was beginning to feel like some kind of divine phenomenon.

"Have you ever been through so long a storm before?" Miri asked Benjamin where they once again watched the storm from the breakfast table. "Six days seems awfully long for a whiteout," she marveled.

But then again, maybe it wasn't? She didn't really know much about snow.

"It is longer than usual," Benjamin said absently, before turning to her, the grin that she found impossible to resist planted on his face. "Are you so eager for it to pass?"

She wasn't, which made the grin and the question feel even more like darts as they landed.

With each passing day, Miri wanted the storm to end less and less, and she knew that was unrealistic.

Since the moment she had taken charge in the sitting area, something had changed in Benjamin, and that change in itself was making it harder and harder for Miri to keep things in perspective.

Since that night, he'd filled their time with the kind of holiday joy and pleasure that was the stuff of movies, sharing every family tradition he could remember along the way and taking her body to heights and places she'd never thought it possible to go.

They'd baked, watched Hanukkah movies in his personal theater, they'd cooked meals that took multiple phases and hours to complete without having to wash a dish along the way, and they'd gorged on fare prepared at request by his personal chef.

They'd made love in the spa—where he'd discovered all those robes so long ago—and in the library and in the hot tub, and the hallway, *twice*.

Each passing day with him was slightly better than the last, and with each one the inevitable end of the storm crept closer.

Miri wasn't sure her heart or head could take the torment of that push and pull for much longer.

Maybe she *did* want it to end now, just to lessen the hurt inevitable when it did.

A storm like this couldn't hold out for the duration of Hanukkah, could it?

Eight days of whiteout was unbelievable—despite the fact that they were well on their way through six.

The end had to be near, could come at any moment really, and Miri wasn't ready.

But what else was there for it?

Her job was the key to her independence and stability. It was the achievement she'd worked years to be ready for and as much as she had come to appreciate Benjamin, she would not give it up for him.

She could not.

It might have been different if there was something else on the table—something real and lasting and tangible, like commitments and family—but there wasn't. She knew now, better than ever, how he felt about those ideas.

And nothing he had said or done had suggested there might be something different about what was going on between them.

No. In fact, if anything, it was explicitly otherwise.

They had agreed on something temporary and secret—and neither of those was a strong enough reason to leave a job she loved and needed.

When the storm ended, she had to return to the real world, where she was just another woman working hard to survive and he was Benjamin Silver.

Her Benjamin had made her into a goddess, placing the world at her fingertips, but that fairy tale couldn't last forever. For all that he was open and revealed, *her* Benjamin wasn't the real one.

The magic that let them playact would eventually end, at which point she would have to somehow figure out how to pretend like it was okay that everything was back to normal.

Normal would never be okay again, not after Benjamin.

Normal didn't even *exist* after Benjamin.

Normal for Miri was virginal and entirely focused on her job.

After six days with Benjamin, she wasn't sure she would ever be able to fully focus on anything else ever again.

The man had infiltrated her consciousness in a way that meant he could never be far from her mind again, and she was growing more and more certain that the end of the storm would bring with it not relief at the chance to finally go home, but unbearable heartache—of a kind she had never known before.

CHAPTER TWELVE

BENJAMIN LAY BESIDE MIRI, listening to her deep, even breathing.

His room was dark still, no sun yet to backlight the snow outside, the sheets entangled around them.

Though he could not see it, he knew that outside the storm continued. By this point he had come to recognize the sound of it, like constantly listening to a muffled ocean inside a shell.

It did not matter that the storm continued, though.

Whether it did or did not was irrelevant to everything that came after. He'd finally realized that, somewhere between her having her way with him on the couch all of those nights ago and waking now, fully alert in the darkness beside her.

He could not let her go.

It was utterly ludicrous and ridiculous that they both acted like it was even possible—or necessary.

They were modern adults, neither of them indentured to the foundation or under any obligation to let it dictate their personal lives.

In this day and age, it was incredibly rare to meet someone who it was possible to work alongside, laugh with and reveal deep fears to, and in Miri, he had found all three. He had risked being vulnerable with her, made himself vulnerable to her derision and mockery, and instead she had chased away the shadows in his heart with her heat—as powerful as the light of any fire.

It wasn't the kind of thing any sane man would walk away from—one didn't give another the power to break them and then just go their separate ways—especially not because of a set of rules that had never been intended to apply to him.

What he had discovered with Miri—honesty, openness, passion and safety—was far bigger and more valuable than even the foundation.

Only a fool would pretend otherwise, and he was no fool.

He was one of the most powerful men in the world.

At his side, Miri stirred.

"Quiet down, over there," she murmured, her voice as sleepy and soft as her body in the shadowed room. "You're thinking so loud, it's waking me up."

"I don't want to end things when the storm ends," he said. He had a reputation for being blunt.

Beside him, she sat up.

"What are you talking about?" she asked, though he knew she knew.

Just like himself, he'd caught her looking out the window, eyebrows drawn together in a frown, multiple times over the past few days and he knew it was because she was afraid to see signs of its end.

He couldn't be the only one feeling that.

"There's no reason we can't continue to see each other after the storm passes," he said.

She shook her head, and he felt the reverberation of it through the bed they shared.

"No, we can't. The foundation…my job. We can't. I could get fired," she said, sounding tired now whereas she'd sounded sleepy but alert only moments before.

"No one needs to know," he insisted.

She scoffed. "Just like with the last events director, huh? No. No. We both know it's a no. Someone would find out. They always do, and you're famous. I told you, Benjamin. I can't afford to lose my job. I don't want the storm to end any more than you do, but you should know better than to ask me that."

He resented the censure in her voice, even if it was deserved.

She admitted to feeling the same; she couldn't in the same breath speak to him like a child.

"What I'm asking is not out of line, Miri. We're two adults with something good going between them. I'm asking you to give that a chance because I like you."

"But do you respect me, Benjamin? Because right now it doesn't seem like you do. I told you, I *need* this job."

"And if you lose it, I have more than enough money to take care of you until you got a new one. You're a brilliant woman, Miri. You don't need the foundation."

"You'll take care of me?" she demanded, voice rising. "I'm just supposed to put my trust in Benjamin Silver to take care of me if I lose my job? Why would I do that? You're not my dad. You're not my husband. When all is said and done, you're a man I barely know. And like I told you, I *do* need the foundation. I need the foundation more than a man like you is probably capable of understanding, and what's more, I *want* it."

"I *want* you," he snapped, and could swear he heard her mouth shut. "And you want me," he continued. "It's outrageous for us to ignore that because of the foundation."

"And what about because it's what we agreed to do? Or do you want me more than you care about me?"

How could she ask that? he wondered.

Had he not just spent days revealing in small and large ways just how much he cared for her?

He had shared his family traditions with her, for God's sake.

"I want you *because* I care about you, Miri," he insisted. "More than any woman before you."

"Or do you just want me more than any other woman because you can't have me and it's driving you crazy? We had a deal, Benjamin. Only until the storm passes. You wouldn't be saying any of this if it didn't have an expiration date."

He heard desperation in her voice as she spoke but could not decipher its root.

Was she desperate he believe her, or was she desperate to believe herself?

Because there was a question, he could not backtrack.

If she simply did not share the same intensity of desire for him, that would be one thing, but he knew she did.

He saw it in her eyes whenever he looked at her.

He felt it when he was inside her.

But like he had been, she was afraid.

"That's a lie and I think we both know it, Miri. You're afraid."

"I'm not afraid," she rasped. "I'm practical. No matter how many times we make love, it doesn't change the fact that I'm a single woman living in an expensive city. It's misogynistic of you to ask me to put my stability at risk just because you don't want to stop fooling around, but I wouldn't expect you to realize that."

"Misogynistic? Come on, Miri. Don't be ridiculous. We both know that misogyny is the furthest thing from my mind when we touch, just like your refusal isn't about misogyny right now. You're just afraid to get hurt. You got hurt once a long time ago and just like me, now you're too afraid of getting hurt again to tell the truth. You're afraid to put your heart on the line."

She gasped in the dark and for all that he regretted them now, he knew his words had hit their mark. She had wielded truth gently when she'd pointed it out to him.

He'd used it like a baseball bat.

When she finally spoke, her voice was rough. "The only thing I know is on your mind when you touch me is sex, Benjamin. Nothing special or romantic or lasting, just sex. You don't want *me*, Benjamin, you just want to keep having sex with me, and only then until you inevitably get tired of it, like you've gotten tired of every other woman you've had sex with. You said it yourself, you don't want kids, you don't want a family, you don't believe there's a woman out there you can share your burdens with, and you don't want people making demands on your time or distracting you from your work. That means you don't really want *me* because *I* am the kind of person who wants all of those things. You only want me because I'm here. We'd both be fools to pretend like it's anything else. That's why even now you're not asking for anything real or a legitimate relationship. You just want me to continue being your secret lover, your mistress, and you know what, I'm finding that that's something I'm just not interested in." She punctuated the last by sliding out the bed.

Not expecting the movement, he reached for her too late. "Miri, where are you going?"

"Back to my room. I'm suddenly not feeling as comfortable as I was," she said, her words stiff and tight.

Panicking, he swung his legs out of the bed himself, standing on the opposite side of the bed from her, as naked as the day he was born. "I'll walk you," he said lamely.

He didn't need to see her to know she shook her head. The negation was clear in her voice. "I'll find it on my own, thanks. I know the way by now."

"Miri…" he started, but didn't know what else to say.

"What, Benjamin? Am I wrong? Did I get the wrong impression here? Are you asking me to be the kind of woman you can share your traditions and start a family with? Do you want me enough to commit to more than sleeping together? Are you willing to risk loving me?"

All of the peace and heat and certainty he'd felt lying beside her, listening to her breath—along with his own breath—fled him.

Abruptly clammy and chilled, the sinking in him now an echo of what he'd felt upon learning of his family's death, he reached an arm toward her voice in the darkness but could do no more.

Because he was not.

He could not.

The idea alone shot him back to the day in the hospital, waking up alone in a way he had never imagined he would be again.

He wanted Miri, was crystal clear on that fact, and more than he had ever desired a woman before in his life, but he could not risk that. Not again.

He wouldn't survive a third time.

As much as her words cut through him now, he could not fathom what it would be like to lose her after falling in love with her.

He said nothing.

When his pause had lasted long enough to become its own answer, she said, "Storm or no storm, I don't think we should do this anymore. I don't think it's—" Her breath hitched and the sound of it tore through him. "I don't think it's good for either one of us," she finished in a rush. "I'd like to leave as soon as possible."

He listened as she padded to the door then, cracking it open and slipping out without another word.

And because it was the way his life worked, when the sun rose on the eighth day of Hanukkah, it brought with it blue sky.

CHAPTER THIRTEEN

STANDING AT THE WINDOW, the curtains open, Miri pressed the intercom buzzer in her room as soon as she saw the first sliver of blue sky.

Benjamin wasn't the only one who could call his assistant.

Miri just hoped it worked out like she wanted it to.

It was a huge relief to hear the woman's voice crackle through the wall speaker—even if the crackle had more to do with the woman speaking than the intercom her words traveled through. "What can I do for you, Ms. Howard?" she asked.

Rubbing her palms against her thighs, clad again in the skirt she'd worn to meet Benjamin for the first time, she said, "I noticed the sky had cleared and was wondering if it would be possible to return to LA today?"

"I'll have to check with the pilot," she said, disappearing for a long few minutes while Miri continued to watch the sunrise.

She had not returned to bed upon leaving Benjamin's room.

There was no point; she couldn't sleep.

Not with their conversation fresh in her mind.

She supposed she should have been flattered that he wanted her to be his mistress.

He was a world-famous sexy billionaire who had changed the world and who was she?

She was a woman who was not going to act like a fool because a man was good in bed.

Maybe he wasn't even good in bed. She had no comparison—because he had been the first man, unlike every other man she'd ever met, to make her feel safe enough to let her guard down.

Her heart squeezed in her chest with a steady, painfully rhythmic beat.

He was asking her to put her fate in his hands, for no other reason than he *wanted* her.

The universals of womanhood transcended even those of faith, and she knew how much store could be set in what a man wanted in any given moment.

Or what anyone wanted of her in any given moment.

Whether it was her former fiancé's want of her as a mother of his children, her family's want of her to celebrate their way, or Benjamin's want of her to be his mistress.

Wasn't it all the same thing?

In none of those cases had she been wanted as a partner and cocreator. In their own ways, each of them had made that clear.

But she didn't have to wait around at the whim

of anyone's capricious wants. She owed herself as full a life as she'd challenged Benjamin to live. She deserved a family, and shared traditions, and commitment.

And she would go out and get them.

Even if it wasn't with Benjamin.

The knot in her chest threatened to stop her heart from beating altogether.

Excruciating as it was, she didn't know if she didn't just want to let it.

She let out a strained gasp at the sound of Benjamin's assistant coming back to the intercom. "Pilot says there's not enough runway to fly you home yet, but he could probably get you to the airport in the chopper."

A helicopter.

Of course, it would have to be a helicopter, and then a commercial flight after that, at best.

Commercial flight at best? Where did such a thought come from?

Now she was incredulous with herself.

Just a week with Benjamin and she was already disdaining regular air travel?

She could handle a short ride in a helicopter. The vast majority of helicopter flights made their itineraries, and she was obviously losing her grip out here with him.

And the time it took to get through the airport and home would give her time to adjust to her reentrance into the real world, where she had no idea what it was like to make love to Benjamin Silver and women like her moved slowly and deliberately through quiet lives.

"I'll take it. Thank you," she said, her cadence more like a sob than a sentence.

That was fine, too. There was no law against crying on planes.

"Sounds good, miss. He'll get it fired up. Probably be about thirty minutes till you're in the air."

Thirty minutes.

She could handle that.

It was short enough that she could tell herself there wasn't time to say goodbye.

It was barely enough time to pull herself together enough to make the trip.

Twenty minutes later, Benjamin's assistant drove a bundled-up Miri to the helipad in a snowmobile.

Even temporarily clad in outerwear from his incredible wardrobe, with hat and gloves and all, it was too loud and cold for either woman to have brought up Benjamin.

Did he even know she was leaving?

Miri assumed he did. His assistant reported to him, after all.

If he did know, he didn't come for her.

Outside, what had been a thin layer of snow when she'd arrived was now a transformed landscape.

Forests had disappeared, replaced by mounds

and hilltops of sparkling powder dotted with only the tallest of frosted trees.

Benjamin's gargantuan mountain cabin needed only enormous gumdrops to have transformed into a massive gingerbread house, its immediate vicinity and walls kept clear of snow by what looked like some kind of ground-based heating, while its thick-beamed roof lay covered with even thicker sheets of bright snow.

It was so cold outside that it was almost hard to breathe, but the deadliness of the chill did nothing to diminish the beauty of the wintery landscape.

Miri was amazed.

She had never imagined that snow could be so beautiful, the storm that had created a world of its own for Benjamin and her leaving behind still yet another new wonder to explore.

It invited one to do classic winter things like sled and build snowmen and drink warm beverages but only when it was time to come in from playing—things Miri hadn't spent much time thinking about before, but now would forever regret having missed the chance to try.

Benjamin had ruined everything.

He'd ruined her disdain for the cold and winter and snow, just like he had ruined good wine and doughnuts and probably Hanukkah, too.

Thank God she'd gotten what she needed from him for the gala, otherwise he probably would have ruined that, too.

That she would have to face him again at it certainly constituted a level of ruin.

Though she wore a thick jacket meant for the snow, she was shivering by the time they reached the helipad.

"Think you're going to want to keep that on for the ride. It's not bound to be the warmest today," Benjamin's assistant told her when she tried to return the jacket, and Miri sighed.

She didn't want to take anything from him, but she wasn't willing to freeze to death to make a point.

He hadn't known he'd owned it in the first place, so he probably wouldn't have even noticed it being gone.

Tears turned into ice droplets around her eyes as she geared up for the helicopter ride and that, too, was a first.

Ten minutes later, they were taking off.

Miri was glad it was too loud to hold a conversation, even through the headset.

She didn't feel like making small talk.

She felt like burying herself in a dark room and staying there for days. Unfortunately, because of the storm, she'd already done that and now she had to get back to work.

She'd have to hit the ground running for all the time she'd lost, though the work she'd done with Benjamin ensured she could get it done.

Benjamin…

She didn't want to think about him, but of course she had no choice.

Even now, she looked for him, wondering which of the massive windows in his home he stood behind and watched her leave from—if any.

Did he care? Was he angry? Or had he simply gotten back to work?

Watching his home grow smaller, she realized that each option hurt.

The farther she got away from him, the more everything hurt, in fact.

Why hadn't he come to her? Why hadn't he said goodbye? Why hadn't he stopped her?

He tried to stop you, a voice inside reminded her. *By making you his mistress.*

Was it possible to think about him and not end up wounded? she wondered, watching a tiny figure dash from the front of his home.

Moving fast, it made a beeline for the helipad, which continued to grow smaller.

Miri watched, momentarily confused by what she saw.

A figure waving frantically, flares in their hands.

What was going on? Was it Benjamin?

"Stop the chopper!" she yelled into the headset, pointing toward the ground below.

"What?" the pilot hollered, turning to look where she pointed.

Then he nodded, and her stomach did a somersault as he began to turn the helicopter and descend once more.

CHAPTER FOURTEEN

BENJAMIN WATCHED THE helicopter descend with ice in his veins.

He had felt this before, chilled to the bone before he'd passed out in the Pacific and woken utterly alone in a hospital bed—cold, afraid and so painfully alive.

He hadn't thought she would stop.

It was too good to be true.

No matter how much money he had made, he knew not to expect too good to be true.

People didn't come back once you'd lost them.

He hadn't thought she would simply leave, either, nor had he any idea of how much it would hurt to watch her go.

It had been enough to rob him of words and breath, so that he could only respond with agonized grunts and desperate motion, fighting the sensation of drowning even as he ran after her.

She took off into the air while he continued to sink further down below, watching her rise resigned to the fact that he had finally joined his parents at the bottom of the sea.

He'd been so afraid of being broken by losing love again that he'd chased his away.

It turned out it didn't matter what form the loss took, though, it hurt both ways.

Thankfully, this time, there could be an opportunity to do it all better. His decision to live again had given him a second chance.

The Miri that disembarked the helicopter was not the one who had first arrived.

That woman, clad in a thin cardigan and bearing a bright blue box of doughnuts, had been a stranger.

The woman he saw now, bundled appropriately for the weather with her arms crossed in front of her chest, was the woman he loved.

In just eight days, she had sneaked past decades of his defenses and gracefully navigated the minefield of his fears to become someone who took his heart when she left.

Somewhere in the mad dash after her, he'd realized that it was too late to protect himself from her.

He loved her, and because of that, she didn't have to die to kill him.

All she had to do was walk away.

But as long as they were both still living, there was a chance for life.

He wouldn't let fear keep him from the love

that was possible with her, not when there were so many with whom he didn't have a choice.

He owed it to the dead to not squander his opportunities with the living.

"Miri," he breathed her name, and it rang clear through the cold, crisp air.

"What are you thinking, Benjamin? You don't even have a sweater on!" she exclaimed. "You're going to freeze to death. This is Colorado."

And it was true.

He hadn't had time to appropriately clothe himself when he'd heard she was already lifting off.

Hypothermia was nothing compared to losing her.

"I don't want you to leave, Miri."

Releasing her arms from their protective position at her chest, she lifted her hands in the air. "I know. You already said that. You want me to put my job at risk to be your mistress. Well, you know what, you don't always get what you want, Benjamin. Even you."

He didn't flinch at her words; he couldn't. He was too glad she was still here. Instead, he just shook his head, smiling like a fool in the snow. "No. I don't want that either. I want you to marry me, Miri. You were right about what I said earlier. I don't have a right to ask you to trust me. I'm not your husband. But I want to be."

She stilled, like a deer in the sights of a predator. "What?" she asked.

"I want you to be my wife, Miri, and the mother of my children. I want to build a family with you and keep my family traditions alive. I couldn't trust my grandmother's recipes to just anyone, but I can trust them to you. I've made a career out of understanding complex patterns that underlie function and trusting my instincts. I don't need more time to see your beauty or value, just like I can't pretend that you're not everything that I want just because the storm has passed. Losing you now or losing you at the end of a long life together feels the same, and in one case I end up a lonely old fool with more money than I can spend, too scared to have really lived."

"But..." she said, eyes wide and mildly stunned. "The foundation...my job..."

"You can keep your job, Miri. I'll step down from my role with the board citing my need for more time for private business projects, effective immediately. The foundation won't dare reprimand you when they see the endowment I'm going to leave them, nor after the spectacular gala you're going to throw for them. I don't need you to give up who you've worked to be, Miri, nor was this ever about you putting your job at risk or being my mistress. That was your label, not mine. I just didn't want to lose you, Miri. Death isn't the only way love can leave you devastated."

Her amber eyes glowing, she cleared her throat before she said, her voice still thick when it came out, "You're going to have to be a little more direct if you want to start throwing that word around."

She was trembling, he could see it, even through the warm jacket she wore, but would hold her line even through her emotion.

There was that spine he loved so much.

"I love you, Miri. Marry me."

It was so cold outside, he could see his breath, could literally witness the command hang in the air.

And then she nodded. And then she said, "Yes. Yes! Absolutely yes!" and ran to him, leaping into his arms.

He held her there, kissing her, standing barefoot in the thick snow beneath a bright blue sky, the lonely chill he'd always relied on his fires to warm gone.

Until she pulled back, horror in her face, and said, "No shoes and a T-shirt? And you gave me a hard time for wearing a cardigan," as she unwound herself from her coat to wrap a side of it around him, too.

Smiling, he said, "I dress for the occasion, which, in this case, was running as if my very life depended on it. Because it did," and kissed her again.

EPILOGUE

"I HAD A feeling I should have ordered an extra box this year," Miri said, wistfully patting the rounded top of her abdomen with one hand as she polished off the last of the *sufganiyot* from the teal box with the other.

Her husband of almost a year now wisely said nothing.

"There was just no way I could have known, though," she sighed. "Everything is so hit-or-miss right now, and I haven't had them for almost a year, so two boxes felt like too much a risk."

Beyond that, she really didn't need to be eating another box of doughnuts almost entirely to herself, even if she was eight months pregnant.

After spending the first night of Hanukkah with her friends in the city, she and Benjamin had returned to Aspen for the holiday, stopping for doughnuts on the way to their airport.

Normally, doctors advised against a woman in her late stage of pregnancy flying, but Benjamin had allayed their fears by insisting that a doctor accompany them on the trip, and only then after a pre-takeoff checkup and approval. He was concerned of what might happen, on the off chance they got snowed in.

Miri didn't mind. She understood and appreciated it, even. Benjamin would always be serious about keeping his family safe. There was no other way he could be.

And it had certainly been known to happen.

If it did, they would be prepared. He always was.

He was going to be an amazing father.

Miri had no doubts.

He was kind and thoughtful, strong and determined, attentive and adoring.

Everything she could hope for her child and more.

And he had been entirely correct about the foundation's reaction—to both his endowment and her gala.

The endowment had made jaws drop. Her gala had made eyes sparkle.

Not only had she secured her position with the foundation, but she had also earned a reputation as one of the best and brightest on staff—in both mind *and* body, because of the flawless dress she'd worn.

Her Secret Garden gala held the new record for most funds raised, as well as made the front page of the society section in the *Los Angeles Times*.

Offering just the right mix of exclusivity, unexpectedness and photo opportunities, both the press and attendees had had a field day with it. It even briefly trended in top hashtags in Los Angeles.

And to make matters even better, she'd looked fantastic in every photo, the two-toned silver and gold long-sleeved body-contouring dress she'd worn popping and glittering against the all-black attire of the man who refused to leave her side throughout the entire night.

The event was the most talked about thing around foundation offices for months afterward, with many of the large donors going out of their way to let Miri know how much they looked forward to what she would be putting together for them the following year.

Even after the buzz died down a bit, she remained one of the most popular staff members—her dreams of happy hours and work friendships blossoming beyond her imaginings.

And all of the recognition had even come with a little salary bump, too—not that money was something she had to worry about anymore.

Not since she had become the wife of one of the richest men in the world.

They were married a month after the gala and Miri found out she was pregnant the following March. Since then, her husband had hardly left her side, taking out an office building across the street from the foundation so he could work nearby.

Her work necessitated they spend most of their time in LA, but for Hanukkah only Aspen felt right. It was their first tradition, a celebration of their own special miracle that had occurred.

She couldn't wait for their baby to be born, so they could join in the celebration, too.

Of course, by the way they were flipping around in her womb in reaction to the doughnuts, she couldn't exactly say they weren't participating already.

Sighing, she decided that she really should have bought more.

Wrapping his arms around her from behind, teal flashed in the corner of her eyes as Benjamin said into her hair, "I knew," and placed a second box of doughnuts on the counter.

Spinning around in his arms, she smiled up into his laughing blue eyes, and he caught her lips with his.

Heat filled her, as it always did when they kissed. He tasted like sugar and stability and a special world for the two—soon to be three—of them, with no end in sight.

* * * * *